# VISCERA

## SIMON MINCHIN

CLIMBING TREE BOOKS

First published 2021 by Climbing Tree Books Ltd.

Copyright © Simon Minchin 2021

ISBN: 978-1-909172-65-4

Published by Climbing Tree Books Ltd, Truro, Cornwall

www.climbingtreebooks.net

www.simonminchin.com

Cover photo by Alex Bamford

Author portrait by Claire Wilson at LLE Photography

Cover design by Ryan Mcfarlane and Grace Kennard

Typeset by Grace Kennard

For Arri, Beanie and Claire.

Love to all xx xx

# CONTENTS

# THE HEART OF THE SON

THE 'THOPTER flew low over the desert. Its four big fans stirred up a dust devil that swirled and whirled and followed them south into the deep sands and on towards the central massif of the Adrar plateau.

Mark and the two boys were sitting in the crew seats in the back. They could see through to the pilot sitting in the cockpit. Occasionally he moved his hands over the control screens. From time to time he glanced at a dial or flicked an overhead switch. The co-pilot's seat was empty. The other crew seats were empty. The 'thopter rolled gently as the fans tilted to keep the machine flying level as it rode the thermals rising from the sand cliffs beneath them. The sun beat down like a hammer on a copper gong. Even with the aircon running it was hot inside.

They had been flying for hours. They had hours to go.

The clever boy leaned forward and tapped Mark on the knee. He pointed at the pilot then put his hand over the mic on his headset. 'He's not really flying this, is he?' he said. Mark frowned, pulled his headset up and leaned in towards his son. The boy repeated what he'd said. Mark scowled. He put his finger to his lips and mouthed, 'auto pilot'. The clever boy looked back at the pilot and shook his head dismissively. He leaned towards his brother but Mark pulled him back by his elbow. 'Just read your tablet or something,' he said.

The pilot tapped the control on his headset. 'Sorry. I missed that. What did you say?'

'Nothing,' said Mark. 'I was just telling my son that we still have a long way to go.'

'Couple of hours, I guess.'

'You don't know?' The boy's voice was loud in everyone's headsets.

The pilot turned in his seat. 'No landmarks in the desert, kid, and this thing flies itself. It'd land itself too but insurance says I have to do that. Don't know why. She makes just as good a job of it as me.'

'Not really a pilot then are you?'

Mark sank his head into his hands and stared at the grains of sand that blew across the checkerplate floor between his boots.

"Well, that's the thing. I'm rotating out in two months. I'm going to fly private charters. Want to know why?'

'I'd like to know,' said the other boy. His voice was quieter than his brother's. Gentler.

The pilot smiled. 'I've been flying the shuttle route into Atar Station for almost a year now and a month or two ago, middle of a flight, I realised I had no idea whether I was on the inbound leg or the outbound run. Can you imagine? I didn't know if I was pointed north or south. A man needs to feel his life's a bit more worthwhile than that.'

'Why do they even have a pilot then?' said the loud voice.

'Oh, just in case something goes wrong. But nothing ever goes wrong.'

.

Sure enough, the 'thopter flew straight and true.

Every so often they saw animals moving slowly across the yellow desert beneath them. Every now and then they saw a bird riding the thermals through the clear blue sky above. The 'thopter rode on its fans like a boat floating on a gentle swell. Their headsets cancelled out the engine noise. The air-con failed to quite defeat the heat. The softer boy complained of feeling sick but the moment passed.

'We're almost there,' said the pilot. 'You might want to come up and take a look.'

'It's OK. We should keep strapped in,' said Mark but both boys were already unbuckled and making their way up to the deck behind the pilot.

'Boys,' snapped Mark but the pilot cut across him. 'It's OK. It's perfectly safe, and not many people get a chance to see this.'

Reluctantly Mark undid his seatbelt and, hanging on tight to any handhold he could find, walked nervously up to stand behind the co-pilot's empty seat. 'Hold on to something,' he said to the gentle boy. 'Don't touch anything,' he said to the clever one.

'Let's just go up a bit,' said the pilot. 'Get a better view.' He slid two fingers across a touch screen and the engine note changed. The pitch of the fans went up and the 'thopter began to climb. Mark held tight to the back of the co-pilot's chair, his knuckles yellow through his tan.

The pilot pointed through the windscreen. 'Over there.

That's the first of them. Can you see?'

The plateau was rich and rugged. The crumpled lines of far-off mountains glowed purple against the pale sky. In front of them was a vast flat plain of beige and grey. Mark and the boys peered into the distance and at last they saw what the pilot had been pointing to.

Thrown across the landscape like a handful of coins from a giant's hand were eight shining discs. At first they glittered like pieces of silver. Each one the same size. Each one separate from the others. They looked like circles of beaten metal lying perfectly flat on the land. Each had a spot of brilliance gleaming at its centre. It was a god's necklace, broken and strewn across the plateau.

'I didn't know there were so many,' said Mark.

'Well, you know, the government thought, in for a penny, in for a pound,' said the pilot. 'And it seems that building half a dozen up here wasn't six times harder than building one, something to do with experience and infrastructure. But don't get excited. You might have neighbours but those things are big. You couldn't walk from one to the other. Not up here and not in this heat.'

'Which one is us?' asked the gentle boy.

'Over there on the right. The one closest to the cliffs.'

The pilot brushed his fingers across a couple of screens then took the tiny joystick between his fingers and thumb and tilted it forward. The 'thopter responded. The fans spooled up and the body of the machine tipped into a nose-down stance. It accelerated towards the shining disc by the cliffs.

'Go back and sit down,' Mark said, as the 'thopter tilted, but the clever boy slid his bottom into the co-pilot's seat. 'I'm OK here,' he said.

Mark bit his lip. He looked at the boy standing next to him. 'You hold on tight,' he said and the boy nodded.

As they approached the gleaming circle, it changed. A wave of blue ran across its surface until it looked like a perfectly round oasis in the desert. At its centre was a tall column, like a palm tree sitting on a tiny island.

'It's beautiful,' said the sensitive boy.

'That is so cool,' said his brother.

The pilot laughed. 'Cool's the last thing it is. In the middle, at the top there, that's the solar furnace. On a good day it'll hit 3,500 °C. That's… bloody hot.'

'Why did it go blue?' asked the quiet one.

'The circle is made of mirrors. They focus the sun on to the furnace. From where we are, all we see is a reflection of the sky. So they look blue.'

'Our unit's at the base of the tower, isn't it?' asked Mark.

'Uh huh,' grunted the pilot.

'Is that where we are going to land?'

'God, no. If we flew in there we'd end up a flamer.'

The boy in the co-pilot's chair turned and looked at the pilot. 'What's a flamer?' he said.

The pilot chuckled. 'You'll find out.'

.

The 'thopter landed in a cloud of dust, a hundred meters from the outside ring of mirrors. A breeze blew the dust across the desert and it fell in a gentle rain towards the nearest mirror.

'Fuck,' said the pilot under his breath.

Mark looked at him. 'What?'

'I was a bit too close. The dust will get on the mirrors

and you'll... It will have to be cleaned off.'

'They can tell if the mirrors are dusty?'

'Oh yeah. I should have let the bloody autopilot land it. Never mind.'

The 'thopter's doors unlocked and hissed as they slid up into the open position. The hot desert air came crashing into the cabin, brassy and brutal. The air was so hot it felt as if it was burning the hairs right out of Mark's nose.

'My god,' murmured Mark. 'I never imagined it would be like this. We'll never stand it.'

'It's a lot cooler under the mirrors,' said the pilot. He looked at the two boys, walking across the sand towards the mirrors, kicking up the dust with their feet. 'But no one has brought kids before. What's that all about?'

Mark's eyes looked up and to the right for a second. He moistened his lips and rubbed his fingertips with his thumb.

'My partner, their mother, she wanted me to look after them for a while. Her job, it's very... she's... I thought it would be a good experience for them.'

The pilot looked at Mark and shrugged. 'Whatever. It's nothin' to do with me. Surprised they let you though.'

The two men stood and watched the boys as they jostled and shoved like siblings do. They looked like two perfect dolls, two life-size figures cast from the same mold. A pair of puppets made of gutta-percha, brown and shiny and flawless, being tugged through life by invisible strings.

'Nice boys,' said the pilot.

'They are,' said Mark. 'In their own way, they are.'

'Oh here's Jock, look,' and the pilot nodded towards a figure stepping out from under the mirrors. He looked like a Bedouin. He looked like a camel rider. A tall thin man made taller by the soft pile of a turban on his head, the ends of that material wound around his neck like a scarf. His eyes were hidden behind thick green goggles. His cotton shirt and trousers were oversized; they fluttered and flapped in the gentle breeze. On his feet he had sturdy leather boots and around his waist some sort of utility belt. He dragged a small backpack across the sand by its strap.

He ignored Mark completely.

'Let's go,' he said to the pilot.

'Hang on. We've only just landed. These guys…'

'Let's go,' Jock said again. 'This fool's here,' he nodded at Mark. 'That means I can go. Let's go.'

'The boys need to get their stuff off the 'thopter,' said Mark.

Jock lifted up his goggles to see Mark more clearly. 'The boys?' he whispered. Mark nodded and looked towards his sons. The tall figure turned to see what Mark was looking at. 'Fucking hell,' he said.

.

Mark called the boys back and they got their rucksacks and backpacks out of the cargo hold. Mark had his own backpack and hard-shell to unload.

Jock stood off to one side. He would look out into the deep desert, then back at Mark and the boys. He seemed unsettled, like a cat with a twitching tail.

'Get some hats on them,' he said to Mark. 'They can't be out in the day without a hat. And you,' he said scowling at Mark's bare head. 'Same goes for you.' And then he turned back to the desert as if they were no longer any concern of his. As if he was in the air and on the return leg already.

Then he looked back again. 'Why are you all dressed like Boy Scouts, huh?' All three were dressed in khaki shorts and short-sleeved shirts in the same material. They had takkis on their feet and short socks. He turned to the pilot, shrugged in bafflement. 'Don't they get told anything?' he said. 'Don't they get briefed?'

'I just fly them here, same as I did you.'

Mark frowned. 'I was briefed. I did the training.'

'A few days in the simulator, eh?'

'Yeah.'

'And how's that shaping up for accuracy?' said Jock with a little sneer.

Mark could feel the sweat running down his back. Every breath seemed to scorch his sinuses. The heat haze made the mirror supports dance as if they were swaying under water. The top of the tower, where the solar furnace was, shone brighter than the sun. It seemed impossible to look at it.

'What would you say this place is?' asked Jock.

'The Atar Station Solar Project is an ecologically and environmentally safe…'

'Oh, get real,' snapped Jock.

Mark thought for a second. 'The Atar Project brings together Russian investment and Chinese technology in order to…'

'Steal African sunshine and sell its energy to the Europeans.'

The pilot raised an eyebrow. 'OK,' said Jock. 'Maybe not "steal". But you know what I mean.'

The boys were sitting in the dirt in the shade of the 'thopter. The bright one was tapping away on his tablet, the gentle one was leaning on his backpack and listening to the conversation. 'My Dad is going to be in charge of it,' he said quietly. 'He's the manager.'

Jock seemed to be about to laugh out loud but then he caught himself and looked a little sad. 'I'm afraid the AI got that job. This place looks after itself. Your Dad's here for the same reasons I was. The flamers, the fuckin' 'roo rats and to satisfy the insurance company. That's about it.'

'Told you,' said the clever boy, his eyes not leaving his screen.

.

Jock said he'd walk them over to the quad bike that he had left in the shade of the mirrors. The pilot gave them a cursory wave and started his pre-flight checks. 'Don't be long,' he shouted at Jock's back and Jock nodded.

The boys ran on ahead.

'Why did you bring them?' asked Jock.

'I thought we could spend some quality time together.'

'Bullshit. Why did you bring them?'

'It'll just be like a long summer camp. It's an experience.'

'Oh, it's an experience all right. Why are they here?'

So Mark dropped his voice and dawdled a little to let the boys get further ahead and then he told him.

Jock bit his lip and scratched at his cheek. 'Ahh,' he said. 'That's shit.'

'It is what it is. I'm just trying my best for them.' He sighed. 'It's not easy to do the right thing, you know.'

For a moment they walked in silence.

Jock unwound the turban from his head. He screwed the cotton up in to a ball and handed it to Mark. 'Take this.'

'Thank you. We'll be OK.'

'I hope so, man. You've got your biochip key, eh?'

Mark nodded.

'That'll let you in to the system. Well, some of it. There's a copy of my blog on the drive. The password is I-fucking-hate-this-place. All one word. Have a look. Might be useful.'

'What will you do now?' asked Mark.

'Well, as you know, it's good money so what I should do is start a new life but what I'll probably do is whore and drink and snort it all and I'll be back here for another tour.'

'We're here for six months.'

'Yeah, I know.'

They stepped into the shade, stepped through a ruler-straight line drawn through the air; hot and bright on one side, cooler and darker on the other. The boys were climbing all over the quad, yelling with excitement.

'OK,' said Jock. 'Ill just show your dad how the GPS works and then we can all be on our way.

Being under the mirrors was like being in a forest. The mirrors themselves made the canopy, the tree trunks and undergrowth were made from the struts, stanchions and posts that supported them. Hydraulic lines hung down like vines from above and ran across the desert floor like roots.

On a screen between the handlebars the GPS was flashing away. It showed a path through the mirrors to the centre of the rings, to the foot of the tower where the units were, their home for the next six months. The path looked like the concentric rings and broken radius lines of a circular maze. The electric quad was a tiny ball bearing that would roll down a path and around a ring until it had solved the labyrinth, until it fell into the centre. Thinking on what Jock had said, it seemed to Mark that the AI was beginning their relationship by playing games with him.

The boys, of course, thought it was wonderful.

The big electric quad had twin seats and three big panniers and a couple of cargo nets but it was still a struggle to get themselves and all their stuff on to the bike. One boy sat on the rear seat but the other had to sit on the battery and hang his feet to one side and ride sidesaddle. Mark had his rucksack on his back and so had to sit as far forward as he could in order to give the boy behind him enough room.

Just about the same time as they heard the 'thopter take off, Mark twisted the throttle grip and the quad moved smoothly and silently forward. A wobbling pile of people and their luggage, it looked like nothing quite so much as a bunch of clowns riding a toy car around a circus ring.

The path had obviously been well used. There were tyre tracks in the sand, lots of tracks. Mark wondered why people had had to drive around the mirror field quite so much. It was meant to all be automatic.

The track wasn't that much wider than the quad. Just as if they had been riding through a real forest, they could see only so far into the thicket of mirror supports on either side. Dappled light came down through the gaps between the mirrors but it fell in strange, geometric shapes like lasers stuttering down in a nightclub. The light was bright and brutal. It made the shade that much darker, the shadows looked blacker. The quad's electric motors gave a faint, high-pitch whine. The tyres kicked up a low cloud of dust that hung behind them like a mist.

'This is amazing,' said the gentle boy, his eyes gleaming.

'It's bigger than I thought,' said his brother. 'A lot bigger. How many mirrors are there?'

'There are about ten thousand collectors, I think,' said Mark. 'Each one's made up of something like thirty shards.'

'What do you mean? What's a shard?'

'It's how they get the mirrors to focus on the tower. I'll explain later. I need to concentrate on this. We don't want to crash.'

And just like that Mark went cold and clammy and his skin crawled as he ran through in his mind just how bad it would be if any of them got injured out here. He thought how long it would take for a rescue 'thopter to get here, that's if they could call one, that's if the corporation would approve the flight. He wondered how long it would take someone to die out here in the desert under the mirrors; cut off from heaven, from man and god. He swallowed hard and ran through the mantra that he had been taught, the intonation that was meant to stop the stress from drowning him, from overpowering him completely.

He breathed in, and with the breath came some calm. He breathed out and with the breath went some fear.

'We don't want to crash,' he said quietly to himself.

The boys looked at each other. The one in front smiled at Mark. 'We won't crash, dad,' he said. 'We won't.'

.

It took them more than thirty minutes to get to the centre of the mirror field and the foot of the power tower. Mark stopped the quad. He and the boys got off. No one spoke.

The tower was three hundred and fifty meters tall, a polished concrete cylinder that rose up and up into the sky. At its summit was a place where they could barely look. Some shapes that appeared to be a drum and a ring and a cap but were so lit by the sun that they seemed to be made of the very stuff of the sun. As if a piece of our star had been cut out and dragged down to burn like some giant candle flame on the tip of the tower. The brightest, most incandescent light any of them had ever seen or imagined. How had man found the temerity to build this machine that plucked the sun from the heavens and chained it to the earth?

The sensitive boy took Mark's hand in his and held it tight.

The bright boy shielded his eyes with his hand and peered into the burning light.

'You'll hurt your eyes,' said Mark.

'I don't think so,' said the boy. 'They would have said, and they didn't say. They didn't say not to look at it.'

The tower looked like a hole burnt through the fabric of reality.

'All the mirrors,' said the boy. 'That's where they focus the sunlight. All of it is focussed up there.'

Mark nodded but he didn't seem to be looking at the tower. He seemed to be thinking about something else. His eyes were blank and his lips moved noiselessly.

The boy looked puzzled. 'Can we climb the tower?' he asked looking up at Mark.

'No! Don't be stupid,' snapped Mark. 'Never say that.' But he knew the last thing the boy was, was stupid.

'What are all those?' asked the other boy. 'Is that where we are going to live? Which one is us?'

At the base of the tower, taking up about half of the central circle, was a collection of buildings. Industrial. Built to purpose. As if the architect or designer had realised that the solar tower would literally out-shine anything else that was put on site and therefore he or she had settled for practical and workmanlike. There were huge beige and grey concrete cubes next to translucent skins stretched over hooped metal frames. Corrugated steel boxes connected together by molded tunnels and cast plastic doorways. There were two highly polished tanks spewing out a skein of pipework. Almost every building was covered with air-con grills and on the roof of one long unit was an array of PV panels.

'Where are we? Which one is us?' shouted the boys.

'Over there, I think,' said Mark. 'Over by the hydroponics tunnels and next to the salt reservoirs.' He pointed at a square, grey building with a yellow panelled entranceway. It had tiny, slit widows and the roof was covered with air-con units. Butted up against it was a storage container and to one side were a pile of empty drums and the remains of another quad bike that someone had started to take apart and then just left. There was a fuel cell standing on four rickety legs and two big plastic evaporator sails from a pair of atmospheric water generators. It looked to Mark like this had been the last on-site accommodation for the building and testing crews but he'd never expected the accommodation to be five-star.

'It's like a camp,' said one of the boys.

'Can we explore?' said the other.

'Let's get settled in first. See where we are all sleeping and that. I'd like something to drink. Are you two thirsty?'

The boys followed Mark to the yellow doorway. They

carried their luggage. Mark couldn't see any shade parking for the quad and he didn't want to leave it out in the sun.

He pushed against the yellow door and it swung open.

'I guess you don't get many burglars,' said Mark, a comment the boys treated as just another 'dad joke' and ignored.

The yellow pod turned out to be some sort of porch or boot room. There were jackets and capes hanging up on a line of pegs. Some protective gear that looked scarily substantial and plenty of junk; empty drink bottles and a broken pair of goggles and a toolbox and a hardened tablet hanging on a cord and another turban all unravelled and loose.

'Coats?' asked the gentle boy.

'It gets cold at night in the desert,' said his brother.

'Come on,' said Mark. 'Let's see where we are going to be living,' and he hustled them through the inside door.

·

'How are you settling in?' asked the HR guy.

'Pretty good,' said Mark. 'There's a lot to take in. Most of the monitoring seems pretty straightforward but there are a lot of logs in the history files that I can't make sense of. Stuff that Jock was doing but I can't see what it was.'

The HR guy's lips moved but there were no words.

'Your audio's dropped out,' said Mark.

The HR guy tapped his earpiece mic. There was a crackle. 'Is that better?'

Mark nodded.

'So, what were you saying? Who's Jock?'

'The guy before me. The guy I took over from.'

'Oh, yeah. Right.' He looked at another screen that Mark couldn't see. 'McNorty. J McNorty. Yeah. He'd been one of the glitch crew so when he applied for the caretaker job it made sense that...'

'Caretaker job?' said Mark.

The HR guy did a little stutter. He blinked and started again. 'That's the thing, isn't it. I mean with your qualifications you are the on-site manager. McNorty happened to have had experience on Atar but he couldn't run the system or anything like that. That's ridiculous, but you have the knowledge... although the system runs itself. I mean we made that clear, yes? This is a very light-touch job for you. You essentially have to do nothing. Well, the AI will give you a few maintenance jobs but again, we explained that, yeah?'

'Er...'

'We were lucky to get you. We know that. You're way over-qualified but that's a good thing. If it wasn't for the thing...'

'The thing?'

'The thing at Four Solaire. You know what I'm talking about.'

Mark felt himself go cold and still. He rubbed his chin and jaw, his fingers scraping over the stubble. He frowned, but his eyes were scared.

'We aren't blaming you – obviously – but you needed this job and we needed you to do it. But no, for all your qualifications you are just there to keep your nose clean, keep your head out of the control system and do whatever the AI says. OK?'

The HR guy looked pleased with himself, like a man who has navigated a tortuous pathway or completed a tricky task. Juggling perhaps or some sleight-of-hand. He leant back in his executive chair. He seemed to have a corner office. Behind him floor-to-ceiling windows showed a view over the manicured parkland at the corporation's EMEA centre. The sun was setting. It was quite beautiful.

'How are the boys finding it?' The HR manual obviously suggested that you end a tricky vid call with a bit of touchy-feely stuff.

'They're OK.'

'That's good, I mean, we had our reservations about them going along but when you explained the situation, well…'

'I'm going to get them into remote school soon but I guess a week or two won't hurt.'

'Not been any flamers yet, then.'

'Jock mentioned them. What are they? What's a flamer?'

'Oh nothing. They're just a bit annoying. It's still a bit early in the year, I guess.' The HR guy made a show of looking at his watch. 'Listen, I have to go. If you need anything just book in a call and I'll try and take it. Have a nice day.'

The HR guy leaned forward and pressed his control screen. An icon appeared on Mark's screen that said "ending call" and there was a click as the audio dropped out but then, just before Mark turned off his monitor he saw the background to the HR guy change. The corner office and the panoramic windows and the Oceanside view flickered and then disappeared leaving the HR gut sitting in his cheap, plastic executive chair in a cubicle lined with grey material. There was plastic shelving and a filing cabinet and a work roster pinned to the wall.

The HR guy frowned and reached up towards the

camera on his monitor. He touched it and the screen went dead.

.

ASSYST LOG.
JOB CODE 788
MIRROR No LP 9870 RTY
FOCUS CONTROL FAILURE
DEPLOY MAINTENANCE TEAM
HYDRAULIC SUPPLY FAILURE
DEPLOY MAINTENANCE TEAM
URGENT

Mark was woken by the sound of a buzzer. He padded downstairs and sat in front of his workstation. The screen was glowing green and a message was slowly scrolling across it. The Assyst log code looked similar to the ones that Jock had been dealing with.

Mark heard the sound of a door. He turned and saw one of the boys, sleepy eyed and peering through the doorway. Mark waved him back to bed.

'I think I need to go out for a minute. You go back to sleep.'

He turned back to the screen and began asking the AI questions. He already knew the quad's GPS would find the mirror for him but what might he need to do when he got there? What was the problem and how could he fix it? Obligingly the AI showed him a short video of what to do and pointed out that the skill level necessary to make the repair was "minimal."

Through the slit windows he could see that it was barely dawn. The exterior thermometer was disturbingly low.

Mark threw a thick jacket over his shoulders. He grabbed a tablet and stepped out of the unit door and into a brand-new day.

.

Mirror No. LP 9870 RTY looked just the same as any other, which was no surprise to Mark as all the collector mirrors were absolutely identical.

He plugged the tablet in to its control box and ran a diagnostic.

Sure enough, the skills necessary to get to the bottom of the issue were indeed "minimal." The shards the collector was made up of, that allowed the big mirror to change shape and focus its sunbeam accurately, weren't moving. They weren't moving because the unit had suffered a loss of hydraulic pressure.

The only thing he didn't quite understand was why the tablet screen was flashing an "urgent" message and why a big red digital countdown clock was running in the top right corner.

He used the tablet to override the mirror's hydraulic pump and boosted the pressure in the skein of pipes that fed the back of the mirror. Sure enough, hydraulic fluid squirted from three places in the complicated pipeline. He drained the hydraulic system where the leaks were, cut the damaged tube out and then spliced it all back together again. He could see what looked like teeth marks on the tubing. Something had been nibbling at it.

The tablet continued to flash its plea for urgency. Mark guessed it might be some sort of time and motion study. As the sun climbed, the mirrors all around Mark began to flex and rise up to greet the new day. For a second or two, LP 9870 RTY stayed immobile and it looked as if it might foul one of the other mirrors but then it too began to move and joined in the synchronised dance that grabbed the morning sunlight from the sky and threw it against the top of the solar tower.

The clock had run down. The flashing message had disappeared.

While he was loading up the quad and getting ready to run for home, Mark saw three little rodents looking up at him from the desert floor. Black button eyes, huge ears and kangaroo-like back legs. One of then hopped towards a hydraulic pipe, tiny yellow teeth bared. Mark shooed it and its friends away.

So that's what was really needed, he thought; a plumber and a pest-control man. Well, what state-of-the-art power facility doesn't need them?

After a couple of weeks, Mark bulled the boys back to remote schooling. He stripped the data out of a couple of the facility's laptops and adapted a pair of VR headsets he found abandoned by the departing crews. The boys sat next to each other just as they would have done in a schoolroom, two peas in a pod. Mark sometimes found it hard to tell the difference between them; with the VR headsets covering their eyes it was well-nigh impossible.

After a few days of school, he asked them what they had been learning.

'We've done some maths.'

'And I did some trigonometry.'

'That's maths, isn't it?'

'And languages, we did languages.'

'I did French.'

'And I did Python and Golang, but we're doing modern languages next.'

'What did you do today?'

'Yeah, what have you done?'

'I asked dad, first. What have you been doing?'

Mark's smile stiffened a little. He felt it change from a natural state to an expression that was the result of the instructions he was sending out to a dozen small muscles in his face.

'I patched up a couple of hydraulic leaks and blocked up a kangaroo rat nest and swept sand off a few mirrors out by the rim. You know just doing my…'

'I could do that,' snapped the boy on the left. 'I could do that easy. I could your job,' and he turned back to his laptop.

'You should be nicer to dad,' said his brother. 'You should be nice.'

.

ASSYST LOG.
JOB CODE 789
MIRROR No SN 9856 TR4
DEBRIS OBSCURING MIRROR SURFACE
DEPLOY MAINTENANCE TEAM
POTENTIAL MIRROR SURFACE DAMAGE
DEPLOY MAINTENANCE TEAM
URGENT. DEPLOY NOW. URGENT.
Mark thought that "debris obscuring mirror surface"

was a fairly straightforward-sounding problem and so, although the Assyst code was one he hadn't seen before, he didn't ask the AI for any further clarification or advice.

The quad took Mark out to SN 9856 TR4.

From beneath at least the mirror looked fine. There was no obvious damage and it seemed to be still tracking properly, keeping pace and position with the others around it.

Mark pulled the folding ladder off the back of the quad and struggled with it for a moment. He'd used it quite a few times already but the way its joints worked always seemed to defeat him. Their sole purpose seemed to be to trap his fingers and pinch his skin. The ladder seemed to unfold in a different way each time. He imagined that this would be what you got if you crossed a puzzle with a mantrap.

At last, and for no logical reason that Mark could see, the ladder assumed its correct position and stayed there. Locking pins engaged. Joints solid.

He set the ladder up by the side of the mirror.

He pulled a pair of heavily tinted goggles over his face. He hung an extendible scrapper and a brush from his belt. He slipped on a thin pair of nitrile gloves and turned his cap around so that the peak would shade his neck.

He climbed, one rung at a time.

The mirror was just a few degrees off the horizontal. By the time he could see across its surface he was a good three or four meters off the ground and the soles of his feet were itching and his hands were sweaty inside the nitrile gloves. He muttered the intonation against stress under his breath and that helped a good deal.

Where the problem was, was immediately obvious. As to what it was, Mark didn't have the faintest idea.

A black and pink pile of debris. A mound of something shapeless and formless about the size of a man's head. There were smudge marks across the mirror surface around it. There were parts of the thing that looked familiar but what it was in itself, Mark didn't have a clue. And there was a slightly unpleasant odour in the air.

Perhaps it was a meteor. But it would have smashed through the mirror.

Perhaps it was an animal that got cooked on the mirror. But how did it get up there?

Perhaps it had been thrown from a plane. But why?

Holding tight to the ladder, Mark reached out with the scraper and gave the thing a nudge. It didn't budge but a part of it's crusted surface tore and there was suddenly the most sickening stench of burnt flesh and rotting viscera. Mark gagged. He prodded at it again and the thing, whatever it was or had been, moved a little. Mark saw spines that resolved themselves into quills as the thing slid along the mirror. Some of the soot and dust was caught by the breeze and blew away as a tiny cloud of blackened feathers. There was a beak, and a claw.

By the time it was close enough to pull off the mirror surface Mark could see that it was a bird, a fairly large bird. Burnt to a cinder.

What on earth was that all about?

.

'You should have brought it back, dad. I want to see it.'

'It was disgusting, and it stank.'

'But I want to see it. What did it look like?'

'Like a big burnt bird.'

'Like a chicken? Like a chicken that mum's cooked?'

Mark was about to snap out a reply but he managed to stop himself, managed to breathe and pause before he said anything.

'No. Not like mum used to cook chicken. At least her chicken didn't still have its feathers on.'

'Can we call her and tell her? You said that after a while perhaps we could call mum.'

'Yeah. I want to see her.'

'And me. I want to as well. You said we could.'

'I said "perhaps". Perhaps we could.'

'What does "perhaps" mean? Yes or no?'

Mark stood there, blinking. He chewed his lip. He felt as if he'd stepped into a trap and a door had clanged shut behind him and he couldn't see a way out and he felt that now was the time to be honest and just say, just say what had to be said. But he couldn't.

The buzzer sounded on his workstation and another message began to scrawl across the screen, another instruction to go and do something trivial and pointless.

Something menial.

Something much easier than telling the boys the truth, and so he told them to get on with their schoolwork and walked out into the desert.

.

Eventually it was Jock who told them about the flamers.

To distract the boys, Mark showed them where Jock's blog sat on the server and then let them use a set of algorithm keys to break the encryption and crack the security.

'That's rude,' said the gentle one when the blog's firewall finally crumbled under the brute force attack and gave up its password.

'Perhaps he didn't like being here on his own?' said Mark.

'It's still rude.'

Jock's blog consisted of hundreds of hours of video footage, thousands of still images and even some CAD3D design files but fortunately it also had a search function. They got about one hundred hits just on their first keyword search but after a bit more refinement they got down to a dozen files that looked like they might have some information in them rather than just a passing reference. The boys cued them up in a playlist.

The first two were just Jock complaining about how disgusting the flamers were to clean up, and, to be fair, Mark knew that well enough already.

The next file had been corrupted or perhaps something had gone wrong with the recording. The fourth file had what they were looking for. It started with Jock leaning into screen and apparently adjusting the camera until he was satisfied with the image. Then the audio kicked in.

'...fuckin' fiddly little... There. OK. Fine. Just stay there. Oh shit... Oh. OK. That's got it.'

He sat back in his chair and smiled into the camera.

'OK. Here we go. Well, I should tell you the date and all that shit but do you know what, I have absolutely no idea what it is. Hey ho. Who cares?' He rubbed at his forehead and cheeks where goggles had left deep red lines on his skin.

'I do know it's about the beginning of April though because the birds have started to migrate and the reason I know that is because they are dropping out of the fuckin' skies and landing all over these precious mirrors and nubbins here has to go out and clear them up.'

He spat on the floor.

'I mean the 'roo rats are bad enough but we get the flamers as well… Fuckin' crazy. You would think old Mother Nature would be pleased with this place, eh? From an environmental point of view it's a fuckin' triumph. A closed system with no waste products, it only makes electricity. Oh, and thirty-odd million kilograms of molten salt but let's not bother about that. But what does she do? The bitch tries to bring the plant to its knees with dead birds and scabby little rats. Unbelievable.'

He poked around inside his mouth, picking at his teeth. He found something, peered at it then flicked it to one side.

'OK. So. Flamers. All the sites at Atar Station get them. We kept quiet about them because we didn't want the tree-huggers to get in the way of progress or, as the corporation calls it, profit.'

He leaned back and folded his arms, looked down his sunburnt nose into the camera.

'Twice a year, the migration routes go right overhead here,' He pointed up towards the unit's ceiling. 'Millions of birds and most of them are fine.' He sucked his teeth again. 'But some of them are flying a bit low or they want to see what it is we're doing here or they are just unlucky and they fly too close to the solar tower. And they burn.'

Mark looked over at the boys but they didn't seem upset. They looked fascinated.

'The thermocline around the tower is pretty steep. One of the guys called it a thermal flux. It's a ball that surrounds the solar furnace maybe a hundred meters across. In there, the temperature gets to about one thousand degrees. Bird flies into that and they dehydrate in seconds and then burst into flames. Fall to earth like a fuckin meteor. Sometimes one or two at a time but sometimes a flock goes in there and it looks like fireworks night in the daytime, I kid you fuckin' not.'

Jock raised one cheek off his chair and there was the clear sound of a fart. The boys laughed out loud.

'When we were glitch-testing we never ran the tower full hot for very long so we didn't really appreciate the problem. What we got then we called "streamers". Birds would fly in and get hot, maybe even start to smoke a little, hence the name, but they generally got out again and flew off albeit a bit singed. But now, running full power, the tower cooks 'em and burns 'em in seconds and down they come and land on the mirrors and that's the problem. If Atar's output drops below a certain level then the Europeans can renegotiate what they pay for the juice and you can be sure they ain't gonna decide to pay more. That's why the fuckin' AI has me running my ass off keeping those mirrors clean. To stop dead birds eating the profits.'

Sure enough, starting with that first one, flamers became increasingly common as the continent moved into migration season. Thousands of millions of birds flew journeys that ranged from just a few hundred kilometres to trans-continental quests that took them from the tip of Africa to the heart of Europe. Many of them flew over Atar Station and many of those, like a bizarre twist on the story of Icarus, flew too close to the man-made sun and scorched their wings, streaming smoke and flame as they fell on the mirrors.

The AI could sense the light output from each mirror and so could tell Mark what mirrors needed cleaning. There was also a backup system that used drones with image recognition software that tracked the flamers through the sky and found their final resting places. Quite often when Mark got to a flamer he would find a bunch of these tiny, dark drones buzzing around the corpse like mechanical blowflies.

As the number of flamer hits increased, so did the AI's enthusiasm for them to be quickly cleared. Sometimes, Mark spent an entire working day riding from one scrape-job to the next with only a minute or two to face-call the boys and check that they were behaving, that they were studying.

Of course, boys never behave.

The first few days of their new found "freedom" they explored every square inch of the unit, all the rooms they used and all the ones they didn't. They found some interesting stuff that the last construction crews had left behind; some porn, a few half-empty bottles of alcohol, some really cool jackets but most of them too big, broken tech, optical memory discs and a vicious looking knife.

They took their search outside.

Boys assume that adults hide stuff that they don't want boys to find and that the reason they don't want them to find it is because it's really, really interesting and perhaps rude or dangerous or scary or all three. This may well be the case but the boys' three-day-long search of the rest of the camp yielded nothing. There were no drugs growing in the hydroponics tunnels. The turbine and generator halls were securely locked. They couldn't work out how to put the broken quad back together. The lossless power hawsers that fed the electricity off site were buried underground. Essentially, it all seemed exciting, but it wasn't. It was like a system that they were locked out of and they couldn't find a way to break in. And that made the clever one think.

'Let's see what else Jock put in his blog, shall we?'

'He seemed like a nice person, didn't he?'

'Well, shall we?'

'It's like spying on him.'

'No, it's like viewing his blog. That's why people make them. So that other people can see what they thought and that. They want them to be watched.'

'OK,' and they went back into the unit and turned on the big video screen.

The boys started to run through Jock's posts and updates at random. Sometimes he was funny, sometimes he was crying and sometimes he was definitely drunk but mostly he was boring, until they found a post that had an unusual title. '"The most important jobs are always left to the least important people," it said.

'What's this?'

'Dunno. Let's see.'

Jock was sitting cross-legged on the floor in just a pair of shorts and an old vest. He was either drunk or trying to become drunk. He kept drinking from a plastic cup. Sometimes he missed his mouth and spilled.

'People used to worry about the machines taking our jobs. Not me. The machine gave me my job. It's 'cos of the machine, I'm here. Fuckin' thing,' and he slurped from the cup.

'There's the flamers and the rats of course but do you know what, I reckon the machine could sort those things out if it needed to. I don't mean the machine, of course. I mean the designers, the builders, the corporation. Those people. Poison the hydraulic fluid and there wouldn't be a rat problem for long and there are some solar sites that run self-cleaning mirrors. The tech is there. It could be done.'

He drank.

'So why am I here? I'm the person whose fault it is. I'm the one who takes the fall. Listen. Listen. It's true,' and he leant into the camera and squinted down its lens. 'Atar Station powers hundreds and thousands of lives. The power towers are simple and flawless and so can never mafunctio… malfunction. It can never go wrong. But sometimes they do. And so there has to be a man here because any corporation that lets an unmanned site go tits-up is gonna get sued to shit for not having a man there to keep an eye on things. But there's a problem with that.'

The boys were quiet. They weren't quite sure what they were listening to but it was definitely 'adult stuff' and that in itself made it interesting.

'Those clever fuckers who built this place,' said Jock, 'looked at all the accidents and failures and catastrophes that had ever happened with stuff like this and they made a worryin' discovery. The accidents are never due to a failure with the tech, with the software or the hardware. The accidents are almost always caused by the wetware.' Jock tapped his own chest. 'By the soft machine. It's human fuckin' error, every single time. The man pressed the wrong button or threw the wrong switch. He set the wrong code or entered the wrong data. The man fucked up.'

Jock upended the cup. One single golden drop fell to

the floor and then Jock threw the cup away.

'So they came up with a neat solution. Really fuckin' neat. I am here; I am on site but there is nothing I can do here. I have no button to press or switch to throw. Nothing. Not one fuckin' thing. The AI won't ask for my opinion or advice or, never-in-month-of-fuckin'-Sundays, my command. It totally doesn't give a shit about me and there is nothing that I can do to change that. I am pointless.'

He ran his hands over his shaved and sunburnt head.

'I'm not a cog in the machine. I'm just a fuckin' cog.'

And when the smart boy leant forward to switch the blog off, both boys realised that Mark was standing in the doorway and had watched the whole thing.

.

'I knew what the job was when I took it,' said Mark quietly. 'I didn't want to be in control anymore, and everything was already my fault.'

'What do you mean?'

'Just that.'

The two boys moved closer to each other, as if they were in need of support. Mark covered his face with a hand, like a mask. It made his breath sound harsh and mechanical.

'I used to think…' He paused. 'I used to think I knew what was best, what to do. I was wrong.' He looked at the floor, dirt and sand on polished concrete.

The clever boy nodded his head. Tiny, quick movements like a palsy.

The gentle one swallowed hard. Words reabsorbed; concealed. Then, 'You do know what to do, dad…'

'He doesn't. He just does what that machine tells him,

just like Jock. He's stupid.'

'No,' snapped the gentle one, suddenly bright and full of spark. 'No. No, he isn't. He looks after us. He looks after us and…'

'And look where we are. This isn't our home. This isn't where we should be. Where's mum?' The quick one bridled like an angry cat. 'Where's our mum? Why can't we call her?'

'It's not that simple,' murmured Mark.

'Why isn't it?'

'It just isn't. The reason we're here is…' Mark tried to speak but the words became tangled in his throat. His chest tightened. He looked around, a trapped animal looking for a way out. 'I'll tell you. Give me a minute.'

Both boys looked about to speak but Mark held up his hand. 'Just give me a minute. Go to your room. Please,' and he looked so fragile that they did.

For a while Mark just pottered.

He threw the old meal wrappers away.

He put a sanitiser tab in the dew collector's reservoir and checked the levels.

He threw a pile of washing into the machine.

He tried to give his subconscious space in which it could decide what to say.

He listened to the pumps as they circulated molten salt from the hot tanks into the heat exchangers. They sounded like mechanical beasts breathing in the depths of the metal forest.

He put the kettle on to boil but didn't bother to sink a teabag in his mug.

He checked the pump logs.

He took a step closer to the boys' room. He took a deep

breath and pushed the door open. The boys were playing a sim. Mark sat down on the corner of one of the beds. The boys looked at him. Hesitant and nervous like two small creatures stepping out on to thin ice. When grownups broke, worlds shattered.

Mark closed his eyes. 'I was working at a place called Four Solaire. It's a solar tower plant, like this one...'

'No. I want to know about mum. I want to know why she isn't here.'

'I'll get there. OK,' and Mark's voice was so small that the boys sat quiet and listened.

'I was working at a place called Four Solaire. It'd just been finished. All we had to do was glitch-test it and then commission it. I was a design engineer. I wrote some of the code for the solar tracking and... Well, it doesn't matter. I was like an executive or something.'

'When? I don't remember.'

'It was a couple of years ago. We were living in that house with the pool that looked over the valley. Anyway. It was like this place. The AI was in charge. But it hadn't been finished yet so there was an external control patch. Basically, I could override the machine. I was showing your mum around.'

'Not us?'

'You never went there. And this was the last day I ever did.' Mark shivered although it was still hot in the unit. 'She wanted to see how the mirrors moved. The AI was due to start a tracking run in half an hour or something but we were in a hurry. I don't remember why.' Mark took a deep, shuddering breath. 'Dear God, I can't remember why. I logged into the control patch, turned the AI off and moved the mirrors. I focussed one whole array on the tower. It was easy. She said how beautiful it looked, how the mirror field looked like flowers moving in the breeze.' Mark's voice broke, like a child. 'They stopped us on the way back to the 'thopter, told me what I'd done. There had been a glitch crew in the tower, three men just doing their job. Last-minute checks or something.'

Mark was crying.

'They said the men must have known what was happening. They must have seen the mirrors move. They would have felt it start to get warmer. They must have known what was happening but they couldn't possibly get down in time.'

'They burned?' asked one of the boys.

'They vaporised,' said Mark. 'I wasn't charged but there was an enquiry.'

'What does that mean?'

'I wasn't charged with a crime. Killing them was an accident but there still had to be blame and responsibility. It got too much for Gabriella, your mum. Perhaps in some way she blamed herself, perhaps she blamed me, but she just couldn't handle it. It was all hushed up. The corporation didn't want any bad PR, but people talk. People knew what had happened. What I'd done. She said it felt like we were standing on the tower and feeling the air getting warmer and warmer. Knowing we were going to be burned. Knowing it was just a matter of time.'

Mark wrung his hands as if he was trying to wash them clean.

'Two months ago, she told me she was leaving. That she wanted a completely new life. That she never wanted to see me again. And then this job came up. It seemed like fate. A place to hide. A way to relive the past and make it different.'

'We can tell mum she has to come back. We can tell her you're sorry. We can tell her it'll be alright.'

Mark looked at the floor; the dusty, dirty floor. 'You can't. She doesn't want to see you again either. She's gone. She's just gone. I don't even know where she is.'

'No,' shouted one of the boys. 'Get her back. Make her come back.'

'I can't,' whispered Mark.

'Make her come back,' he cried.

'I can't. She doesn't want to see any of us.'

'I want her back. I hate you.'

'It's not fair!'

'I know it's not. I'm so sorry…'

'I hate you. Just go away. Go away.'

With their eyes obscured by tears the twins became identical. One of them scrambled to his feet and ran towards the door. Mark tried to grab him as he passed but he slid out of the way of Mark's hands. A moment later he heard the unit door slam closed and by the time Mark realised what had happened and ran outside his son was nowhere to be seen. He called for him. He called and called but there was no reply. No little figure walking back to be held or hugged.

When Mark finally went back inside, his other son had dried his eyes and Mark was a little surprised to realise that it was the quick one who had run away.

'Is it just us now?' asked the gentle boy and rather than answer that the pair of them just sat on the floor and held onto each other.

·

After a few hours and no sign, Mark was frightened.

When night-time fell and still no sign, he was terrified.

In the morning, Mark and his son got on the quad and started to search.

'We should leave him some stuff,' said the boy. 'We should leave out some food and water and warm things where he can find them.'

Mark looked at him with a questioning frown.

'He's talked about running away before. He might not come back.'

'Do you think he'll try and cross to one of the other stations?'

The boy thought for a minute. 'No. But I don't know if he'll come home so we should leave stuff.'

Mark thought about this for a little while before driving back to the unit and putting some parcels of food and warm clothes together.

Mark had no idea where to look for his lost son so he decided that in going out and cleaning flamers from mirrors and patching hydraulics, he had as much chance of finding the boy as in any other way so Mark did that although he did take the gentle boy with him.

One day. Two days. Three days.

The packages they left were disappearing so Mark knew the quick boy was alive but he had no idea where he was.

On the fourth day Mark was cleaning a flamer off a mirror when a small flock of birds flew into the bubble of heat around the tower. The birds themselves were too small to see from a distance but all of a sudden five plumes of white smoke appeared, travelling through the blue and brilliant sky. The gentle boy spotted them first and cried out to Mark, pointing at the feather-white trails as they began to slowly descend earthwards. After a moment, the birds caught fire; they became shooting stars in the daytime, a meteor shower against a heaven that was blue, not black. The pair of them watched as the five tiny lives ended and their husks fell to the ground.

And suddenly the boy shouted and pointed to something else, halfway out towards the far side of the mirror field. Mark squinted into the glare. At first he could see nothing but the boy was insistent. 'It's him,' he said. 'It is him.'

Mark used the camera on his tablet and zoomed in. They looked at the screen together. There was a swarm of drones hovering around an object sitting on the mirror. The drones seemed confused. The object was a boy and the boy was Mark's son. He sat and watched as the flamers impacted the mirror field and then he slipped his feet over the edge of the mirror and dropped out of sight.

'Let's go. Let's go and get him,' said the boy. Mark knew he would already be gone by the time they got there but they went anyway.

·

The next day, they saw him again, closer this time. A figure standing on a mirror surrounded by a cloud of drones. He was staring up into the pitiless sky, his arms held out as if he hoped to catch the pair of flamers that were falling towards him. They were big birds, crane or perhaps storks.

Mark could see their wings; the flames that roiled behind their falling bodies. They looked like angels thrown down from heaven.

'Hey,' shouted Mark. 'Hey, wait for us. Stay there and wait for us. We just want to talk.' But the boy didn't hear him or chose to ignore him because he waited until the birds had gone over his head, the smoke trailing behind them like incense, and then stepped off the mirror and disappeared from view.

·

The following day Mark and his son searched high and low for the missing boy. They felt that if they had seen him as they had on the last couple of days, he must be somewhere close. If they could see him, they could find him. They had to be able to find him.

The flamers still needed to be cleared but the birds took the pair of them on a random sweep of the mirror field, which was as likely as any other method to put them close to the lost brother.

They searched from dawn till nearly dusk. The sun was a cooling ball dropping towards the horizon. One section of the mirror field had risen up to grab the last few rays of the sun and trap them in the molten salt that flowed through the furnace.

The power had gone from the sun now but, when it was concentrated, it still had enough heat to maintain the thermal flux.

Mark and his son sat on a mirror watching a huge bird fly slowly towards the tower. Its wings were magnificent, wide and tipped with arrowhead feathers. It soared with a majesty that spoke of its absolute confidence in the skies. It was a raptor; a desert buzzard or perhaps a hawk. Its head turned lazily. Perhaps it was scanning the ground for rats.

Mark and his son sat side by side, leaning gently in to each other. They watched the bird in silence.

'It's just like us,' said a voice behind them. 'It's just like us.' A scratchy voice. A voice cracked with thirst and crying.

Mark and his son turned and saw the lost brother standing there. Filthy and scrawny with reddened eyes. He looked like a refugee. He had that haunted look in his eyes that said he had seen things that he shouldn't have, even if they were only the dreams and fears he had found in his own head. Tears had washed the cleverness from his eyes and something else had grown there.

Mark and the boy were frozen into silence.

'The birds are just like us,' he whispered. 'They think everything is fine. They can't see any problem. They don't know what's ahead of them.' He wiped his face and looked at the dirt that rubbed onto his fingertips.

'Watch,' he said. 'Watch.'

The hawk beat its wings and it entered the flux, the bubble of air that was still at a thousand degrees. The sphere of clear, still air that showed no sign of being different, no sign of being deadly.

'And now it's too late,' said the boy, his voice cracking. 'It did nothing wrong. It couldn't see what was coming. It's not it's fault, but look.'

The hawk no longer flapped. Its wings spread out wide it simply glided through the air for a moment and then began to trail faint, grey smoke from the tips of its wings.

'Just like us,' said the boy. 'We fly into things that we

can't see and they burn us. That's what it feels like to me.'

The boy stepped towards his father and his brother. They moved apart for him. Left a space between them that he could fill. He sat down and they leant in towards him, feeling his body between them. The solidity of him made them all complete. Making one thing where there had been three separate souls. They watched as the hawk burst in to flames and, against the background of the dying sun, it fell like Icarus into the sea of mirrors.

'I thought it was your fault,' said the boy to Mark. 'I thought it was your fault that mum wasn't here, and then I thought it was mine. But it isn't. It isn't the bird's fault that it burns, is it?'

Mark slid his arm both boys' shoulders and they sat together and watched the sun sink below the horizon.

# ROVER

FROM THE campsite next door there is a long, winding path that goes through the fields and all the way up to the copse that sits on the brow of the hill. People used to walk their dogs along it. It's called The Dog Walk.

I don't have a dog.

I think about that for a minute as I nurse my mug of tea. It would be nice to have another living thing about the place. I imagine the dog would be pleased to see me when I got up in the mornings. I can understand why people used to have dogs but I don't have a dog.

I don't have anything.

The Dog Walk is becoming overgrown. I know that because I take a walk along it at least three times a week. That's my exercise. That's how I stay fit. I used to visit the gym but of course I can't do that anymore. I used to jog down to the beach and walk on the sand looking at the sea, watching the breakers as they rolled over each other and thundered onto the shore. I used to like walking on the beach but they say you can't do that anymore. They say it's against the rules.

The restrictions don't stop me from walking to the copse and back, though, as long as I walk on my own. That's almost laughable. I'm always on my own.

I never see anyone else on my walk, not a glimpse. The campsite closed two years ago when the woman who owned it killed herself. It was about the time when things began to get really bad. When people started to wonder if there would be a time when there would be no more life on earth; at least, no more human life. That was a realisation that a lot of people found hard to face and I don't blame her for what she did. Perhaps it was the brave thing to do?

My tea has gone cold now.

I'm trying hard not to cry but my lip trembles and my eyes are wet.

I wish I had a dog. A dog would be good.

.

In the night there is a storm, fierce and rather frightening, as if Mother Nature is beating the Earth with a stick to see if she can drive the last errant children out of her garden.

I lie beneath the blankets, curled up in the foetal position. At the height of the storm there is a single clap of thunder so loud that it rattles the windows and shakes the slates on the roof. I pull the blankets over my head and tuck my knees tight to my chest. I hug the pillow for comfort but it gives me very little and it is exhaustion that eventually pushes me down into sleep.

I have no idea what time I wake. I have no desire to know.

The world outside is quiet and still. A pale glow surrounds the bedroom curtains. I assume a new day has begun but try as I might, I can't decide what day it is. Is it a Wednesday or a Thursday? Perhaps it's the weekend? What does it matter? What difference does it make? This new day would be made in the image of yesterday, they always are.

.

I get dressed and go downstairs for breakfast. There are only three more meals in the delivery pack so it must be nearly the end of the month. I need to log on and update my order or the drone won't know what to drop off for me. There isn't much choice anymore though. It's just been dried and canned and frozen stuff for almost a year now. I can imagine a vast warehouse somewhere that is being slowly emptied, robots picking stuff of the shelves and loading up the delivery drones. At some point I guess the shelves will all be bare and I have no idea what happens then. Well, I can guess, but I try not to think about it. I won't let myself starve to death. I won't do that.

.

To get to the Dog Walk there is a bridleway that runs alongside my garden. It's a sunken lane, a holloway, and in heavy rain it is a torrent. Last night's rainwater would have run down here like a river. Today, the path is slippy. Not just muddy; it's more like trying to walk on silt. The warmth of the sun doesn't penetrate this dark-green tunnel but simply being out in the fresh air feels good. The rhythm of my footsteps is calming even when they slip and slide on the muddy ground.

I feel better.

I don't feel as bad.

I feel OK. Mostly OK.

The sunken lane climbs the hill until it reaches a rusty stile and a set of granite steps. I'm careful over these. I daren't begin to imagine the consequences of taking a bad fall. The irony of that thought makes me laugh. I tread carefully anyway.

I don't choose to die just yet.

On the other side of the stile the path emerges through a thick hedge and into a pasture speckled with hogweed and ragwort. There is a strip of shorter grass that is the Dog Walk; it keeps close to the hedgerow before disappearing into the next field through a broken gate. There are rabbits in the field. They see people so rarely now they have forgotten that I should be treated as a threat. They nibble the grass without giving me a second glance.

Looking back over the way I have come, I can just see my cottage through the trees, the greenhouse that I no longer use, the old well that's boarded over, the collapsed pergola that has fallen into the pond like the bones of some dead thing. Nature is claiming my garden back and it seems I'm not trying to stop her.

I stride out towards the copse, a tight group of twenty young beech, their straight and slender trunks bursting together into green leaf at the top and looking more like a single organism than a collection of separate trees.

At least that's how they normally look, but today they look otherwise.

·

Half of the trees are smashed and shattered.

Caught on the highest branches, an enormous piece of red and silver material hangs down over the broken limbs and splintered trunks. The material flaps and rolls in the breeze like cheap gift-warp over a broken present. It trails across the ground to a brown pit stamped into the field. The crater must be two meters deep. There is rainwater in the bottom; a pool of liquid mud. There are broken fragments of granite and schist and a black tree branch. Whatever made the crater is no longer there. I walk up towards the trees following cables that snake across the grass. When I get to the copse I pick up a length of the material. It's unusual, a metal mesh or metallic snakeskin that is light and strong. The breeze comes up and gets underneath it. It swells, inflated by the wind and I can recognise what it is. A canopy. It is the canopy of a parachute. The cables are suspension lines leading down to what had been the payload. The chute had been meant to lower something gently to the ground but it had obviously all gone wrong. Whether the storm had been too fierce or it had simply snagged the trees at the last moment before landing, something had hit the ground harder that it was supposed to.

But whatever it was had survived the impact. The payload harness was empty. There was nothing in the impact crater.

I chew on a fingernail while I try to puzzle the thing out.

What it was.

Where it is now.

This is a huge parachute for a heavy payload, or a particularly delicate one.

Was it military?

Was it foreign?

Was it from outer space?

And with that I sat down on a chunk of splintered tree. Thinking was hard work, especially if you hardly ever did it.

.

Whatever it was, astronaut, alien or pile of junk, it wasn't here anymore. Which meant it must have gone somewhere.

But where?

The wind dropped and it was utterly still and quiet.

I could hear my breathing and the silence in my head.

A nerve ticked in my left arm and my hand twitched.

My eyes felt heavy.

I zoned out. The world went away or I went away from the world, one of the two. The nerve ticked again, my arm jumped in the air. Startled, I opened my eyes and then almost immediately shut them. I took a deep, deep breath and came back to the world.

That happened a lot these days. Just zoning out. I think it might be the isolation and the loneliness. It might be a lack of sleep. Poor diet perhaps? Maybe it's the thoughts of self-slaughter or just a lack of stimulating conversation? It's hard to tell. Not that there is anybody to tell, of course. Not a single soul.

I walk back to the crater and look down into it again. This time, amongst the mud and the rock, I see there is something else. The broken tree branch wasn't a tree branch, it looks more like an articulated arm or leg, about a metre long, black and shiny. I would say it was an oversize insect leg if it wasn't for the fact that one end of the casing is broken open to show a hint of gears and tubing and broken metal or plastic. The other end tapers to a point, a little foot or claw. I wonder about climbing down into the pit so that I can get a better look at it, but why? Now I can see the leg, I can see the marks the thing made clambering out of the crater. I can see where that tapered foot and others clawed at the earth. At the edge of the pit are marks in the earth where the pointed claws had sunk into the soil. I looked around but there isn't a track I can see, just wet grass and bedraggled weeds.

I take some pictures on my phone; the canopy in the broken trees, the harness and the cables, the broken leg in the crater. I can look at them later and know I hadn't imagined it all. I could do that at least. Or I could send them to someone. Send them to someone to prove I hadn't made it up. I should call the authorities and report this but there aren't any authorities anymore. All the emergency numbers go straight to voice mail or deliver some pre-recorded advice on staying safe and I don't think anyone has recorded any helpful suggestions as to what to do in a situation like this.

.

I decide to walk back through the campsite.

I am absolutely sure that there are no aliens wandering about the countryside but having said that, the path through the campsite is through open ground and if there are any aliens following me I'll be able to see them a good way off.

The campsite looks like overgrown parkland dotted with the wreckage of static caravans and mobile homes.

Some of the statics have fallen apart as if they were giant cardboard boxes left out in the rain. They have buckled and folded and finally slumped to the ground. Caravans have fallen off their wheels or been blown over in last night's storm or one before. One static has been peeled completely open to show its mildewed curtains and stained wallpaper to the outside world. A tree has fallen across two mobile homes, folding them both neatly in half. Brambles run everywhere. A few of the caravans have acted like misused greenhouses and literally exploded with the force of the brambles growing inside them. I walk through all this on a concrete roadway that is just starting to be broken up by saplings and weeds breaking through to the surface. It's an eerie landscape and I'm not sure it was such a great choice for my route home. The brambles are like coils of barbed wire in a war zone. The breeze makes the dead caravans creak and groan like ghosts.

Out of the corner of my eye I see movement.

Something crosses a patch of open ground, emerging out of an overgrown hedge and disappearing underneath a caravan. I don't see it clearly, just a sense of something dark and quick.

I looked around for a stick or a branch to use as a weapon. I had never felt threatened by anything that lived around here but there was something about the way it had moved that worried me. In all the time I had been here I had seen rabbits and deer even the odd badger and a few hedgehogs but something about this felt alien and wrong.

Suddenly a stick didn't seem like a good enough weapon.

.

I had a good idea of the layout of the campsite.

A few hundred meters further down the roadway from where I stood was the swimming pool surrounded by a high wall and next to that, the maintenance shed where the groundsmen had kept their tools. They both seemed like better options than standing out in the open.

I kept my eye on the spot where the scuttling thing had disappeared. It didn't look as if anything was moving down there in the shadows beneath the caravan so I backed off some more and then turned and began to walk briskly away.

I hadn't gone more than a few steps when, pushing out through the brambles, something stepped out onto the concrete path. It was about a meter high and sure enough, it stood on six, or rather five, articulated legs. Its body looked like two crash helmets glued together; curved and panelled and shiny and in the middle of its body was a round bulge with a single glass eye, a lens, looking out from it. The spider-thing shuffled sideways so that its eye was pointed directly at me. I could hear the faint hum of a motor as the eye zoomed in towards me. It screeched and whistled making random electronic noises like static on a radio. I took an uncertain step backwards. The thing took two very deliberate steps towards me. It rocked slightly as the missing leg threw it off balance.

I turned and ran.

Or rather I stumbled and tottered and limped. This was more exercise than I had attempted in the best part of two years. My knees clicked and felt as if they were going to drop me to the ground. My ankles felt weak and unstable. My arms flailed like windmills.

I risk a glance over my shoulder. The spider-crab is

keeping up but it isn't gaining. I might be unfit, but my pursuer has actually lost a limb. I can hear its metal claws clicking on the concrete of the roadway and the crackling, hissing sound that it's making. I put my head down and make a last effort to get to the pool before it catches up with me. I turn a corner between two huge fir trees and the pool is right there behind a high concrete wall and a pair of big wooden doors. I fall against the doors, gasping for breath and my knees scream at me to sit down, but I can't do that. The crab-thing stops and its zoom-lens eye pokes out towards me again. I take a step to one side, edging along with my back against the doors and the thing takes a sideways step to follow me. I can hear the whining whistle that it is making. Its claws clatter on the concrete when it makes little sideways steps as I try to squirm away from it. It looks like a crab and moves like a dog and makes a sound like a broken radio. I take a step backwards but that brings me up hard against the doors and although a lot of the wood is rotten and crumbling the bit that I have my back to feels solid enough. I inch my way along one side, my palms flat against the doors, feeling for a weak spot.

The crab-thing keeps its telescopic eye on me and shuffles sideways, following me along the doors.

My hand closes around something. It feels like rusty metal; a tube, a spike, a post, something that I can swing anyway. I hold it tight, give a little tug just to make sure it will move and then swing it at the thing in front of me as hard as I can. It is a spring rake, a wire rake for sweeping up leaves. The tines of the rake hit the crab-thing low on its side and tangle with its legs. It tries to take a step backwards but then slumps over on one side and thrashes for a second, trying to untangle its legs from the wire tines.

I take my chance and run towards the maintenance shed.

The shed is the size of a small barn. Wooden doors that are wide open, light filtering down through holes in the roof. There are hand tools in racks along one wall and two ride on mowers and a little tractor parked up against the other. As soon as I am in the barn I look for something to use to defend myself and there is a sledgehammer leaning against the wall just inside the door. Without thinking I grab the handle as I stagger past and swing it in an arc behind me. I feel the jar in my hand as the head of the sledge hits something, although what it is, I didn't see. It makes the sound of metal on metal, almost like ringing a broken bell, so I guess it has hit the thing. The momentum of the hammer spins me around and I can see I had hit indeed hit it. The force of the blow has thrown the crab-thing against the shed wall and it is entangled in a pile of netting. Its off-pitch keening has stopped. As it thrashes its legs, trying to get free, it makes a whistling noise that goes up and down the scale like someone trying to tune in a radio.

I swing the sledgehammer back over my shoulder and take a step forward. The thing is still caught in the wire, its legs thrashing, but it can't get purchase enough to move. It slews over to one side and its lens catches sight of me and recoils at the hammer, cocked and ready for a crushing blow.

The whistling changes pitch again until it turns into something that almost sounds like speech. Then it changes again. 'No.' A human voice comes from the crab-dog. 'No don't break it. Don't do that.' The shock roots me to the spot. I lower the hammer until the haft rests on my shoulder. The thing moves very slowly as if it was trying not to startle me. Its lens retreats back into its shell and the iris opens wide in what actually does look like fear.

'We don't mean you any harm,' says a voice in a mid-Atlantic accent. 'We just need your blood.'

.

We sit outside in the sunshine, the spider-thing and I. It folds its legs beneath it quite neatly and watches me through its single glass eye.

Something in its audio has been damaged in the crash landing but the blow with the hammer has knocked it back into place.

'This thing is really complicated', says Dorsey. 'It's no surprise it goes wrong in weird ways.

The voice is called "Dorsey" and the thing is called "Rover".

'It's an acronym', says Dorsey when I ask him why. 'It stands for Remote Operated Vehicle Something Something,' and we both laugh. I tell Dorsey that I thought it moved a bit like a dog and her agrees. 'It's got a bunch of different programs in the AI and one of them is a dog.' Apparently the Rover has to be capable of autonomous action otherwise the signal lag from Dorsey could become large enough for the thing to just freeze, so it has various on-board modes to keep it moving if Dorsey's control signal drops out. Dorsey is sitting in front of a computer screen in Norway.

'The virus can't handle the cold,' he says via the Rover. 'If you are within a few degrees of the Arctic Circle, you're basically safe. The rest of the world hasn't been so lucky. It went airborne,' he says. 'It was bound to, but it still came as a one hell of a shock when it happened. Forget wearing a mask and washing your hands and taking Vitamin D every day. One day about three years ago we woke up to a world where one of the new strains could exist outside a host basically forever. The vaccines didn't work. No one believed that full airborne was possible, until it was too late. People started dying in really big numbers and that never stopped.'

We sit quietly for a while listening to the birds and watching the shadows as they move across the ground.

'So when does it get here then?' I ask.

'What do you mean?'

'This new super airborne virus. When does it get here? How long have I got before I'm infected?'

'Oh,' says Dorsey. 'That happened almost two years ago. You are infected. The virus is here. The air is thick with it.'

Wide eyed I turned to look at Rover. Its single eye looks back at me and blinks. 'You've got the virus and you aren't dead. That's why I'm here, or rather that's why Rover is here. You're immune. You can save us all.'

For want of a change of scene, we go and sit on the edge of the pool, looking down at the broken tiles, leaves and branches that litter the bottom of the pit. There is the desiccated corpse of a fox in one corner, something that had fallen in but hadn't been able to claw or scrabble its way out. The body is still there, pretty much in one piece. Nothing will eat a fox.

'We found you quite easily once we started looking.

It was your groceries. Dead people don't buy groceries. In fact we found eight people still alive in the whole country. Eight people like you. Eight people who have some form of immunity.'

'Am I the first you've contacted?'

'No. It took us a while to get Rover ready to go off on his own. Two of them killed themselves before we were ready.' The glass eye zooms out a little; Dorsey is watching my reaction to this news. I just sit there.

'One died in an accident. Well, you could call it that. He tripped and twisted his ankle. He couldn't move, died of exposure at the bottom of his garden, fifty meters from his own back door. We watched it happen on the satellite surveillance.'

'Not having much luck, are you.'

'A Rover got through to another one of the eight last month as it happens. They agreed to give blood and so that should be being sequenced now. Perhaps it's time our luck changed.'

I look down into the bottom of the empty pool, look at the fox and wonder what its last thoughts had been. Had it given up and just lied down to die or had it never stopped jumping at the wall until it couldn't jump anymore.

'What's this about giving blood? You are taking me back to Norway or wherever, aren't you?'

'We can't,' said Dorsey. 'Rover is designed to find you, communicate with you, take a blood sample and send the DNA scan of that sample back here via a satellite uplink. That's all the tech we got. We can't come and get you. The virus is airborne. The whole atmosphere is thick with it. We just can't risk it.'

'You're leaving me alone here?'

'We can stay in touch till the batteries die.'

'How long?'

'It's keeping this comms link going that takes the power so maybe a month, maybe two?'

'What if I say no to giving blood.'

'Then you will die alone knowing you are the worst man in the world.'

I purse my lips and look at the fox.

.

I tell Dorsey that I need some time alone to think, that I need some space. Can you imagine how weird that is? More than two years of total solitude and just two hours after having someone to talk to again, albeit a talking crab-dog called Rover, I tell my sole companion to leave me alone for an hour or two.

I retrace my steps through the campsite. I go back to the Dog Walk.

I suspect Dorsey is following me although I told him not too. As a walking potential antidote to the extinction of humanity, I think I'm too precious to be allowed out on my own. I guess the other side of the coin is that they could have given Rover a Taser and just taken all the blood they wanted. Perhaps if an antivirus was found and the world began again it would be a better world than the one it replaced or perhaps they just haven't shown me the Taser yet?

The rabbits are back in their field. They look at me as if I am an alien; an out-of-context problem, something they no longer understand or indeed need to. Nature would be perfectly content with the whole place to herself and I hold that thought for a time.

Yesterday I was considering killing myself; today I am wondering whether to save the world. Both those thoughts are far too big to fit inside my head. People's thoughts should focus on smaller things; their wants should be more prosaic.

And I remember the last thing that I thought about wanting and I smile.

Decision made, I walk back towards my house, which is where I had agreed to meet Dorsey and let him know what I have decided. I don't think my choice was ever in doubt. I just needed to feel that it was something I had decided to do rather then doing without thinking.

And if I could negotiate a little exchange and trade, well, so much the better.

.

The morning is bright and clear and stunningly beautiful. A little steam rises from my mug of tea as I stand outside my back door in the chill air.

There is a small, dark circle on the tip of my finger where the lancet had pierced me and from where I had given Dorsey his blood. The Rover had sequenced it and the results had been uplinked and received in Norway. That was about the last thing he said to me before we severed the comms. Keeping the communication link open was just too heavy on batteries and although it would have been nice to hear a human voice from time to time Dorsey had said that Rover might run for a couple of years on his internal power cells if the uplink was disabled. To have a companion for two years was much better than having a conversation for just a couple of months.

I whistle and Rover emerges out of the shrubbery in my overgrown garden. He bounds towards me; five legged, one glass eye but every movement shouts dog.

He jumps up at me like an enthusiastic puppy. He can't bark yet but Dorsey is going to write a little piece of audio software and download it to Rover, which should fix that problem.

Dorsey got his blood and I get a dog. They put the dog persona in his AI in sole control and tweaked a few of the parameters. I get a dog that's pleased to see me when I get up in mornings; a dog that wants to fetch sticks or chase rabbits. I can understand why people used to have dogs and now I have a dog.

Rover is jumping around in front of me, his glass eye fixed on my face. I have a stick hidden behind my back. He's so excited because he knows I'm about to throw it and shout, 'Fetch.'

# SIMON MINCHIN

# HARVEST

THE WOMAN made her daughter breakfast every day. She made it on the days the girl went to school and she made it on the days she didn't.

Today there was a speckled egg and a piece of thick toast and a tumbler of creamy milk.

The woman watched as the girl ate her egg and drank her milk and slipped the slice of toast into her book bag. As usual, the woman said nothing because, what could she say?

The girl looked at the kitchen clock. She gave her mother a sad, apologetic smile and scooped her book bag up off the chair beside her. She folded her jacket over the bag; showers came out of nowhere at this time of year. The woman lent to give her daughter a kiss but the girl slid off her chair and darted for the door as quick as a startled fawn. She stopped on the threshold though and gave her mother a brief, bright smile.

That was something. At least that was something.

.

The girl picked her way across the yard. The hens ran around her, rocking from side to side as if they were clockwork toys. She passed the cow barn and breathed in the rich, sweet smell. She passed the pigsty where the animals could have been molded from the brown, glossy mud. She passed the hay barn, that was almost empty, and the big shed where that dreadful thing sat; red and cold and malevolent.

She made her way towards the top field, stepping carefully as she crossed the lower pasture, which was both their cow's larder and their toilet, and headed toward the five-bar gate in the far hedge. Climbing the gate as if it were a wooden ladder, she held tight to the top rail and leaned out over the golden grass like a figurehead on the prow of a ship. The clouds puffed out their cheeks and blew across the hay. The stalks and stems swayed and ripples ran through the field like currents across a brass and copper ocean. She dropped her school bag onto the far side and looked around before bundling her skirts in one hand and swinging her legs over the gate. Now she ran quickly up the side of the field, running a track that she herself had made but looked like the path of a badger or a deer.

Soon she would actually have to set off towards school if she was to be there before the bell. She only had a few minutes to spare this morning but these moments were precious to her.

Halfway along the hedge she stopped. She knelt down and peered into the hawthorn, bracken, bramble and gorse that made the hedge. She made no sound but her head slowly bobbed and weaved on her slender neck. She moved like a snake sensing something in the grass. She made a little noise, her tongue pressed behind her teeth.

She saw movement in the hedge.

The girl smiled. A broad, happy smile that crinkled her eyes and curled her lips. For a moment she was apple-cheeked and bright as she offered the piece of breakfast toast to her friend.

.

The woman sat for a little time after her daughter had gone.

She put the dishes next to the sink but didn't really see the point in washing them.

She sat at the table, not blinking, hardly breathing and with one hand rubbing at the other.

The clock ticked, but she already knew that time was passing.

She sank her head into her hands, as if her thoughts were getting heavier and she could no longer support them. It felt as if she was crying but her eyes were dry as dust. She looked out of the kitchen window at the white clouds sliding across the blue enamelled sky. At last her eyes settled on the calendar pinned to the wall next to the stove. There was a picture of a cow proudly wearing a rosette, the name "Graham & Ragle" above an offer to supply feed and grain, and beneath that were all the months; last month, this month, next month and the others. If you lived on a farm then nature's calendar was what drove you. Such a thing to be done this month and then that must be done by May. Seeds to be planted by March. Crops to be sown. Hay to be made.

The woman thought on this for a time.

Hay to be made.

For almost sixteen years the woman had lived on this

farm. Since before her daughter had been born she had milked the cows and fed the chickens, mucked out the pigs and planted the seed, tended to the bees and harvested the crops. She had done all these things, performed all these rituals, danced this dance year after year, but she had always had his hand to hold. Always with his arm around her, and now she did not. Now there was just her and her daughter and the cows and the hens and the pigs and the crops and the hay.

She looked at the calendar again. July had passed. August had begun. Nature was marching on. There would be autumn and then the winter months.

The woman sighed.

Winter was not the enemy but winter could be cruel. Winter culled the weak.

If we don't get the hay in, the animals might starve. Most certainly, they will suffer, she thought. We need the hay to get us through the winter. We all do.

She stared at the stone-flagged floor and quietly spoke the words that were in her mind. 'Can I do it without your hand to hold? Can I?'

·

The old man watched the girl from the lane. He took a walk along there every morning. In the past he went with his Collie but last year the dog died. The lane is a public right of way but the old man thought of it as 'his'. His land lies on one side, her land on the other. As if a woman can work her own land. Bloody stupid idea that is, he thinks to himself. Daft.

The old man smelt of tobacco. His white hair had a

yellow tinge. His left thumb was stick-like, the digit replaced with a piece of rib and some scarred skin, a testament to the surgeon's skills and the danger of farm work. His tweed jacket appeared to have been woven from the very stuff of the hedge he was looking over. On the lapel was an enamel badge in the shape of a crucifix. The old man attended chapel every Sunday but none of the other parishioners liked him very much.

He used his walking stick to bend down an errant bramble so that he could see the hay field and the girl. The seed heads swayed and bobbed, a low and murmuring congregation. Thistles stood in clumps, spined and spiked; cruel mementos of Golgotha.

It wasn't perfect, he thought, but it was a good, big field of hay. Five acres. Maybe more. One thing to grow it, thought the old man, but another thing to cut it and dry it and bale it. If it didn't get to the barn then the woman would have a hard time of it in the winter and might be a bit more amenable to his suggestions. It would be nice to own the land on both sides of his lane.

The old man smiled and rubbed his nose with the back of his hand.

.

That evening the woman and the girl sat together quietly after their supper. The girl seldom spoke. It was as if she only had so many words inside her and so she was careful to ration their use.

The woman was at the stove, stirring sugar into water. The girl was picking the stalks and leaves out of a basket of fresh raspberries. Glass jars waited by the sink to be filled with fruit and syrup.

'It'll be good to enjoy these in the winter,' said the woman. 'They'll taste of sunshine.'

The sweet smell from the syrup filled the small room.

'We'll have to do it, you know,' sighed the woman. 'If we don't at least try I might as well sell the place now. Him over the lane will buy it. I don't know where we would go.'

'Then let's try,' said the girl. The words come out of her mouth like round, heavy stones; stones she had kept in a pile somewhere down below. They made her mouth round as the sound of them slips out from between her lips. She puts a raspberry into her mouth and looks at her mother, wondering. The fruit is still a little bitter.

'We'd have to decide when to cut. That was always his job. We cut when he said.'

'Ask,' and the girl nodded her head towards the lane, towards the man who lived on the other side of it.

'No. No, he'd laugh at me. Can't you hear him laughing? I won't ask him.'

The woman took the syrup off the heat and sat down opposite her daughter. She took the girl's hand.

'The weather has been good but it can change fast at this time of year. We need four or five good days to cut and dry the hay. Even then, I don't know. We'd have to get the tractor out and put the mower…'

The girl snatched her hand away. Some of the fruit was knocked to the floor. The girl's brow furrowed and she wrapped her arms across her chest. She hugged herself.

'I know,' said the woman. 'I'm sorry. I'm so sorry.'

.

The girl lay in her narrow bed looking out through the window at the darkening night sky. The blankets had been pushed to the floor. Only a thin sheet and her nightgown covered her. Even in the cloud-dappled moonlight it was warmer than a spring day. Thoughts flooded her mind, a stream flowing over boulders; some thoughts sparkled while some were peat-brown and dark.

She could see two things must be done. One was easy, the other was as fearful as facing down a bull.

·

The girl was up early in the morning. She did her chores, fed the hens and the pigs. The clouds from last night still wrapped the world and kept it warm but they also threatened rain. Mother and daughter stood together in the yard and looked up at the heavy sky. There was no breath of wind.

'I don't know how he did it, your father,' said the woman. 'A lot of farming is about the weather, but haymaking? Haymaking is a dance where you and Mother Nature have to be hip-to-hip in step. When you get it right they say that you have bailed the sunshine in and the hay is sweet and fragrant. Get it wrong and it rots in the barn before winter even comes. Your father had the sense of when to cut and when to bale. He could smell rain on the wind. We never lost a field of hay. Not a one in all those years.'

The girl looked up at her mother, the woman smiled. 'I will have to guess. Or perhaps there is some of him in you? Can you dance with Nature too?'

The girl washed her face and hands before sitting down to

breakfast. While her mother had her back to her she stole a piece of honeycomb from the jar and wrapped it in her cotton handkerchief.

With her book bag bouncing against her hip, she waved to her mother from the kitchen doorway and then sped across the yard and out towards the gate that led to the fields. As always she avoided looking at the dark shed and the obscenity that sat inside it.

After scrambling over the five-bar gate, she ran along her trampled path until she came to that point in the hedge where she stopped. Kneeling, she gently offered the honeycomb, oozing golden ichor, towards the hedge. She made little sounds of encouragement until she saw movement deep in the thicket of gorse and bracken.

'Here,' she said, pushing the honey into the hedge. 'But I need your help.'

.

The woman decided to get the tractor out of the shed while the girl was at school but she still put it off as long as possible constantly finding dust that needed dusting and straw that needed sweeping. Eventually, finally, at last there really was nothing else for her to do.

The tractor was swathed in shadow at the back of the big shed. A missing slate in the roof let a shaft of sunlight spear down to the earth floor. Dust motes and midges span through its brilliance then disappeared into the black.

The tractor looked at her. The woman looked back.

Of all the things in the entire world this was the thing she hated most and yet here she was, dependent on it. Forced into conciliation in order to survive. Why was it the women who were always left to compromise, she thought? Why must we be the ones that back down?

From the front, there was something insect-like about the machine. A deep, louvered grill looked like mouthparts and headlamp eyes bugged out on either side, spindly and jointed front legs splayed out into wheels. It was an iron locust. It was a steel cicada. It was all the woman could do not to turn away but she walked into the dark instead. The dark of the barn and that other dark, the one she tried so hard to hide from.

Like all monsters, the tractor liked to change its shape. When she stood by the side of the machine, the woman saw it as the corpse of a beast; a wild hog perhaps, bestial, brutal and cruel. The massive spine of the transmission ran from front to back. Levers and pedals jutted from it like ribs picked clean. The cab and bonnet had begun life as bright, Massey Ferguson red but they had faded into a pink, the exsanguinated colour of flayed meat. The tractor had lived a hard life.

She swung herself up into the cab, climbing inside the iron beast.

He'd taught her to drive it. She had learnt from him how to change the implements, how to connect the PTO, which lever moved what. She remembered his big strong hands, as confident on the tractor and its machinery as they were on her body.

Remembering him, she remembered what to do and the starter motor turned over and then the big, old diesel kicked and coughed and she moved the throttle a little and the engine settled down to an unconscious heartbeat, as slow and heavy as a funeral drum.

.

The old man leant over the gate. 'You should have done this 'ere couple of days ago. You gone and missed two good drying days, but never you mind, girl. You cut 'en now and you'll be fine.'

The woman had attached the mower to the back of the tractor and pulled it out in to the yard. She hadn't heard the old man coming along the lane or seen him. If she had she would have gone into the house before he could speak to her. He was just a few yards from her now, looking over the gate and sucking on his pipe.

It had taken her the best part of the afternoon to attach the mower, a long arm edged with dozens of triangular rusting blades like un-brushed teeth. Setting the mower onto its tractor mount, she had skinned her hand and her forearm was stained black with dried blood. She pushed the loose hair from her eyes and smeared blood across her forehead. A tribal marking. War paint before battle.

'Should have had this cut Tuesday, I would have said. Your John, he would have known that.'

Bitter bile came into the woman's mouth. He could say what he liked about her, but to bring her husband in to it, to even speak his name; that was beyond the pale. She swallowed her pride and it burnt its way down her gullet making her voice hoarse. 'I'm sure you're right,' she said. 'But he's not here.'

'No, well, neither he is.'

They both looked up into the deep blue sky. Fine, white wisps of mare's tails flicked across it. There was a slight breeze.

The old man nodded towards the mower. 'Do you want

me to check the…' He saw the expression on her face and he plugged his mouth with the stem of his pipe and turned on his heel.

.

When the girl came home from school the tractor was still parked in the yard. It was the first thing she saw; red and malignant, like a tumour. It punched all the air out of her chest and left her rocking.

The kitchen door banged and the woman came out, marching purposefully towards the tractor.

The girl took a step forward into her mother's path. 'No,' she said.

The woman smiled sadly. 'Oh my baby. Don't worry. I know it's hard for you but nothing will happen. I promise you, I'll be safe. Nothing will happen at all.'

The girl looked down at the ground, the earth. It made her think of burial. She shook her head, just the faintest movement, then, 'No. I mean don't cut the hay. Not today. Not today,' and she took her mother by the hand and led her back into the farmhouse.

Once they were sitting in the kitchen, the woman questioned the child but her daughter was resolute. She was adamant that hay wasn't to be cut yet. She would give no explanation nor would she waste her precious words on saying why. The problem was a knot that the woman couldn't tease apart.

At length, they sat quietly, just looking at each other and it was then they realised that what had been silence outside was silence no longer.

The two of them went to the kitchen door and opened

it. They opened it on to a warmer and muggier afternoon. The high mare's tails were now lower and streaming across the sky. The first drops of rain had begun to fall.

Rain.

'How did you know?'

The girl said nothing.

.

The girl rose early the following morning even though it wasn't a school day. She fed the pigs and the chickens. She collected the hen's eggs and left them in a basket on the kitchen table. The woman thought there weren't quite as many as there should have been but perhaps the weather had put the birds off laying?

She called the girl in for breakfast but she didn't appear. The air was oppressive. The yard was still glossy from last night's rain. The tractor was still damp.

Perhaps I did leave it too late, she thought. Like the old man said, it should have been done at the beginning of the week. It hurt her to be wrong, to have let everyone down. In the barn across the yard two calves looked up from the remains of last year's hay and chewed the cud while they stared at the woman with sad, soft eyes. I should have looked after you all better, she thought. The woman stood at the kitchen door drying her hands with a tea towel, rubbing and rubbing and rubbing.

Through the window she saw movement in the distance; her daughter walking across the pasture. She seemed full of energy and purpose. Dew and rain on the green grass made it sparkle. The girl's feet kicked the grass dry and she left a wake of darker green behind her.

'This afternoon,' said the girl. She nodded her head for emphasis, big up-and-down movements. The woman looked at her. She looked up at the sky, grey and dark and heavy. She felt the moisture in the air.

'I think we might have left it too late,' she said. 'John always got the hay in as soon as he could. I think perhaps we missed our chance.'

'This afternoon,' the girl said again and she looked up into her mother's eyes, making sure that she was believed.

.

The woman and the girl pretended to spend the rest of the morning doing the jobs that needed doing. They brushed, they swept they scraped and scrubbed. They put scraps in buckets and feed into troughs. What they were actually doing was watching the weather.

But they didn't need to watch it, the weather was all around them, the weather surrounded them. The clouds had dropped down low and their thick grey blanket seemed almost close enough to touch. Sometimes they felt spat on by tiny drops of rain and sometimes, fat pearls of rainwater tumbled down on them from above and yet the girl kept smiling.

They went indoors for lunch.

There were hunks of fresh-baked bread with some cheese and butter straight from the churn. There were apples as well. The water from the tap was as cold and clear as truth.

'I'm going to put the tractor away then,' said the woman.

The girl shook her head.

'I know you were trying to help. I know you want it to clear up, but it won't. It's going to rain and that's that.'

The girl leant down towards the tabletop so that she could look up out of the kitchen window, Her eyes smiled. She reached out for her mother's hand and, once given, she led her mother to the kitchen door.

The solid cloud had broken into pieces and patches, a crazy paving of grey with a soft and gentle blue showing behind. The air was no longer so close. Along the edge of the top pasture they could see the trees in the hedge moving in the slightest of breezes. Even as they watched, a ray of sunshine pierced the cloud and the darkness began to lift.

Now, it was the woman's turn to be without words. Mother and daughter simply held each other and watched as the afternoon turned bright and dry.

.

The old man watched the tractor circle the field. The mower blade was lowered and stuck out to the side. The woman ran the mower tight up against the hedge line making sure that no hay was left to waste. As the blade swept through the tall grass the hay fell like a breaking wave.

Much to his surprise, the old man found himself giving her a tight and grudging nod of approval.

It was mid afternoon. The woman had waited and waited and bet on the sun coming out and the breeze coming up and it had. The old man understood that. He'd lost count of how many crops of hay he'd brought in and he still got that tight little thrill when he decided to cut.

The woman had cut the edges and now she turned the tractor into a long, stretched-out, figure-of-eight that was the most efficient way to work the field. The old man sucked on his pipe. Well, he thought, she had seen it done before often enough. What was it that they said; monkey see, monkey do, but somehow the thought seemed mean-spirited, even to him.

It took more than an hour to mow the field. The sun beat down with the force of a flail but the woman didn't stop and the old man didn't move.

At last it was done.

The old man waved from the lane gate. The woman wanted to ignore him but it felt just too rude to be that impolite. She drove over and pulled up to a stop just in front of him.

'Decided to cut it, then.' said the old man.

She just looked at him. How did men get to be in charge, she thought? Really. How?

'You done a reasonable job, 'though I might have cut a bit closer myself,' he said.

She bit her lip.

'You want to get it baled up,' he said. 'This weather won't last.'

'John used to say that it needed turning a couple of times first.'

'Hmm. Maybe, but if it get rained on when he's on the ground you'll never get un dry again.'

'I'll have to think about that and see,' she said but what she thought was, I wonder what my daughter will say?

'Well,' said the old man. 'Don't say I didn't warn you,' and he turned and walked slowly away.

The woman went back to the tractor and swung the big

mower bar up into the air to drive back. She was annoyed by the old man's words and even more by his attitude and perhaps she wasn't concentrating. When the mower dropped into place her left hand was still underneath it and the heavy bar slammed down on the back of her wrist. The pain was dreadful but she bit down hard and refused to give the old man the pleasure of hearing her cry.

.

The next morning the woman's hand was purple and swollen.

'Is it broken?' asked her daughter.

The woman shook her head. 'But I can't move it. You'll have to turn the hay. You'll have to drive the tractor.'

The girl looked as if a pit had opened up in front of her. 'I can't,' she said. 'I can't.'

'It's OK. I can show you how. It's not so difficult.'

'No,' said the girl. 'I can't,' and she ran upstairs to her room.

The woman thought for a moment. Things always seemed to work out better if she left the girl to come to her in her own time so she pulled a chair from under the kitchen table and took it outside. She sat in their little kitchen garden with a towel over her knee and her wrist in a bowl of cold water in the hope that the swelling would go down. The sky was full of clouds. They gleamed in the morning sunlight like crumpled satin. She needed to get that hay turned. They needed to get it in.

.

More than an hour passed before the girl came downstairs and sat down on the grass beside her mother. Bees droned around them sounding fat and contented. Sometimes they heard the piglets squabbling over a particularly tasty scrap. The two calves chewed noisily. The woman was wise enough to remain quiet. She waited.

'I saw Dad.' The girl let out a breath; half sob, half sigh. 'I saw him.'

'I don't understand. What do you mean?'

'I saw him die,' she whispered.

The woman frowned. 'Oh baby,' she said. 'You didn't. He was dead when I found him. Don't make it harder than it is.'

'He told me to be quiet. He told me shush.'

'Are you making this up? Please don't.' She paused, then, 'Do you think he's been telling you when to cut the hay and…'

'No,' the girl spat. 'This is why I couldn't tell you. This is why. This is why I had to keep it in.'

The woman took her daughter's hand and squeezed it tight. 'I'm sorry. I'm sorry. Just tell me.'

'The hay, the weather, that's… that's something else.' The girl looked into her mother's eyes in that same way she had before. Needing to be believed. Needing to see the belief. And then, 'I was coming back from a walk. Coming back through the top field and I saw the tractor in the gateway and it looked wrong.'

The woman sat very still.

'I don't know why. It just did. It was too close to the gate and I couldn't see Dad anywhere and the tractor… it just didn't look right.'

Tears began to well up in the woman's eyes.

'When I got closer, I could see him. He was between the wheel and the gate.'

'He was shutting the gate behind him. The brake must have slipped off.'

The girl couldn't look at her mother anymore. She stared at the ground. 'He was on his knees. The wheel was pressed into his chest. He couldn't move.'

'The tractor rolled back and crushed him. He didn't have a chance.'

'He was looking at me. I was about to scream but he put a finger to his lips to shush me.'

'Why?'

'I don't know.'

'And is that why you... you don't like to talk. '

'Yes. It was the last thing he asked me to do. He told me to shush.'

The woman held tight to her daughter's hand.

'I wanted to help him but I didn't know what to do and then the tractor rolled back a bit more and there was a dreadful noise. Dad... he just, he just shivered and then... I didn't see him move again. I ran. I should have done something but I ran.'

'No, don't. Don't say that. Don't you dare say that.'

For a time there was nothing to hear but the bees and then, 'I found him at lunchtime,' said the woman. 'In all the panic and with the police and ambulance and everything I don't think I even noticed that you weren't there. I'm sorry. And then... you never said. Well, you didn't say anything for a long time, did you?'

The girl gave the tinniest of smiles and she squeezed her mother's hand even tighter. 'If we don't do the hay, bad things will happen, won't they?'

'We need it,' said her mother. 'We need it for the winter.'

·

The woman had managed to bring the tractor back to the barn and left it standing outside the shed.

'It's just metal,' she said. 'It can't be good or bad. It's just a thing.'

The girl didn't look so sure.

'We need to get the mower off and put the turner on.' The woman pointed towards the hay turner sitting at the side of the barn. It looked like the skeleton of a fairground ride, the bare bones of a waltzer. Two wire wheels on a frame. 'We'll drop the mower where it is then just back the tractor up to that.'

The girl was trying to breathe.

'You can do it,' said her mother. 'I'll be right by you.'

'I'm scared.'

'You have to be scared before you can be brave. Do you want some breakfast first?'

The girl seemed startled. She looked up at the sky, half grey and half blue. 'There's something I need to do. I'll come right back, but...' And she turned and ran for the kitchen leaving the woman standing there, her hand throbbing and her heart pounding.

A minute later the girl burst out of the kitchen and ran across the yard. She had something wrapped in a tea towel held tightly in her hand.

She must have been gone for no more than ten minutes but when she returned she seemed somehow different. She was quieter and calmer.

They hugged each other.

'I've been thinking,' said the mother. 'Perhaps we should ask for help. Perhaps we should ask him. You know, our neighbour.'

'We can't. We need to do this. We need to do it for Dad and if we can do it this year, if we can do that, then we can do it for always,' and the girl smiled, a big loving smile for her mother.

'But we don't know what the weather is going to do. I can't tell. Can you?' The woman paused and looked closely at her daughter. 'Can you? You can, can't you?' She squatted down in front of the girl. 'How do you know? Where did you go just now? Who did you see? Is it a boy? Have you been seeing a boy?'

The girl actually laughed. Her mother was shocked. She had never thought to hear that sound again.

'Not a boy.' She shook her head. 'It's not a boy.'

The woman wondered what it was then, but she said nothing.

'If it stays dry for two more days, is that enough?' asked the girl.

The woman nodded. 'I think so.'

The girl took a deep breath. 'Then show me how to drive the tractor.'

They dumped the mower where it stood in the yard. They struggled with levers and pedals and gears until the tractor was where they wanted it. The woman remembered watching John put the turner on and she and her daughter brought that memory to life with skinned fingers and banged knees and only three working hands between them. Heavy and dirty and oily, the tractor slowly gave up its secrets. That fits on to there. This connects with that. What had begun by being impossible became at least practical and then eventually became done. The woman showed the girl the clutch and the brake, the gear lever and the throttle.

The first time the tractor jumped forward and stalled.

The second time the tractor lurched forward and stalled.

The third time the tractor just stalled.

On the fourth time the tractor lurched but kept running and the girl managed to turn the steering wheel and point the machine roughly where she wanted it to go. She even got it to come to a stop.

'I'll walk up with you and show you what to do,' said the woman. 'It'll be fine. It's easy. Just driving around in circles.'

.

'Who's driving the bleddy tractor then?' asked the old man.

The woman jumped. She hadn't heard him walk up behind her. 'My girl,' she said.

'Why?'

The woman held up her bruised hand.

The old man winced. 'Ouch', he muttered.

They watched the tractor for a while. The wire disks spun and threw the hay up in the air. The tractor was in the middle of a cloud of dust and hayseed and diesel smoke.

'It's not natural,' said the old man.

'What?'

'A girl driving a tractor. Just a slip of a girl. Bad enough when you were doing it.'

The woman shook her head. 'She seems to be doing all

right. Perhaps it's in her nature?'

'What does she know about nature?' he snorted.

'She's been telling me when to cut and when we need to be baled by.'

'Who's been telling her then? 'Appen there's something else in her nature. Some boy, I shouldn't wonder,' and he took a long draw on his pipe.

The woman looked coldly at the old man. 'What's that on your jacket?' She pointed to his enamelled badge.

'It's the cross of our Lord Jesus.'

'I'm surprised he lets you wear it,' she said and strode out across the field leaving the old man standing as dumb as a fence post.

.

The field was a cloth of gold thrown over the land. The turner had spun the hay into a thick blanket. The hedges around the field framed it beautifully and the sky above was full of little fluffy clouds.

A buzzard screamed in the sky, shrill and somehow pitiful.

Mother and daughter felt the wind at their back and they felt the temperature drop. They turned. Across the other side of the valley the sky was dark and ominous.

'Oh no,' murmured the woman.

'Don't worry,' said her daughter. 'It'll be OK. It'll blow over.'

'How do you know?'

'I just do.'

'But how?'

The girl smiled. 'Perhaps the same way Dad knew.'

'It's in your nature, is it?'

'Something like that.'

'Can we turn it once more,' she asked. 'Do we have time?'

'I think so. How is your hand?'

The woman held up her injured hand. The bruising looked worse but the swelling had gone down and she appeared to have more movement in it.

'Come on then. We'll do it as soon as its warmed up in the morning.'

.

The following morning, breakfast was a specked egg and a piece of thick toast and a tumbler of creamy milk. The woman watched as the girl ate her egg and drank her milk.

'Eat your toast as well,' she said. 'You'll need the energy.'

She smiled to see her daughter looking slightly flustered.

'It's alright,' said the woman. 'You can take this,' and she pushed a piece of cheese wrapped in muslin and a gorgeous red apple across the table towards her. The two women laughed, like women who share a secret, even if they are not totally sure what that secret is.

'I'll turn the field and then bring the tractor back here.'

'Will you be alright on your own?'

The girl picked up the apple and the cheese. 'But I won't be on my own,' she said and ran out of the door.

.

The tractor was all sharp corners and heavy things that moved and turned, rattled and banged but it didn't scare her anymore. She sat astride the transmission. There was only one gear lever that her mother had shown her and she used only one gear. The hand throttle moved stiffly. The engine turned over so slowly that she could hear each cylinder separately from the others; the tractor marched forward to the steady beat of its own drum. The turner whirled like a top flinging hay to either side as she circled the field. The steering was so heavy that she had to turn the wheel with both hands. It felt more as if she was steering a boat than some land-bound contraption. But the field was getting turned. Turned into one continuous pile of hay, a spiral pattern that was both Celtic knot and maze. A labyrinth.

She wondered if she was being watched from the dry bracken; bright eyes looking out from the hedge.

.

When she was finished she drove the tractor back to the farmyard.

There were clouds and those clouds were flat on the bottom and the girl knew that meant rain. She knew that without having to ask.

She left the tractor outside the shed and went in to the farmhouse to find her mother.

'It's done,' she said. 'Just one more thing to do.'

'The biggest thing,' said her mother doubtfully. 'It is the biggest thing.'

'Yes, but I think we can do it. I really do.' She sat herself down at the kitchen table. 'How is your hand?' she asked.

'It's getting better. It doesn't hurt so much.' Then she sat down opposite her daughter. 'How are you?' she asked.

' You seem happier. You talk… you talk more and you have been so brave,' and the woman gave a thin smile.

'We can talk afterwards,' said the girl.

'After it's baled.'

'After it's in the barn.'

'I've been trying not to think about that.'

'The three of us did it last year,' said the girl.

'We had him.'

'And we've got each other now.'

.

The woman's cry was full of such anguish and despair that the animals in the yard froze stock-still and the birds should have tumbled from the skies.

The baler was the biggest machine in the shed. It was a big box on wheels with a rake at the front that would have scooped up the hay and a chute at the back that would have delivered the bales but the baler wouldn't be bailing this year.

When the women began to pull the baler out they discovered a problem. John had partly dismantled the baler's gearbox. There were cogs and pulleys in a pile on the barn floor and two drive belts hanging on a hook on the wall.

'That's that then,' said the woman. 'He must have been replacing a belt or servicing it or…' Her voice tailed away.

'Perhaps we'll be all right? The winter might be mild? We could…'

There was a knock on the shed door and the woman spun around on her heel. The old man was standing there, just outside the barn, his stick in his hand, the end resting against the barn door.

'What?' shouted the woman. 'What do you want? Have you come to gloat? We tried. All right? We tried and we couldn't quite… We almost did it. We tried so hard and…' and the woman began to quietly sob. The girl wrapped her in her arms and glowered at the old man.

'I just…' He bit his lip and tapped his pipe against the barn door. 'I was in the lane when I heard you. I just wondered if there was anything I could do to help,' he said quietly. 'Is there something I could do?'

.

The old man had a baler and he had two sons. Beneath a darkening sky and snatched from under an incoming storm the hay was baled. The bales were thrown on to the bale trailer and brought in to the barn.

The girl worked next to the boys. At first that was awkward but when they saw how hard she worked they began to show her respect.

The woman and the old man stood in the middle of the field. She nursed her bruised wrist and he leant on his stick and drew on his pipe. The heavens turned black above them.

The wind stiffened to buffet them now and it drove the rain before it.

'The bales are getting wet,' said the woman.

'Not enough to do 'em owt harm,' said the old man. 'We're going to just make it. We're going to be fine.'

They walked over to one of the last few bales lying in the field. The old man reached down and pulled out a handful of hay. He rolled it in his fist then held it up to his nose and took a deep breath. 'Good and sweet,' he muttered. 'You made some good hay there.' The old man smoothed his hand across his baldpate. 'C'mon. No point in us getting wet. Let's go and get the kettle on for them workers,' and the pair of them walked back towards the farm even as the sky blackened and roiled and the storm broke above them.

It rained during the night. It rained hard but the hay sat warm and fragrant in the barn and the women slept soundly in their beds.

.

By the morning the rain had passed.

'Dad used to tell me all these stories,' said the girl to her mother as they walked up towards the top field. 'Stories about the sprites and spirits that lived in the woods and the hedgerows.'

The woman smiled at a memory. 'He used to tell me stories too.'

'Sometimes stories are a way of telling the truth, aren't they?'

'Oh yes,' and the woman gave an earthy laugh. 'Yes they are,' and the two women smiled at each other.

The gate to the hay field had been left open. The field had been scraped clean.

'We are going to be all right,' said the girl.

Her mother squeezed her hand. 'Yes. I think perhaps we are. Now, are you going to tell me why you have brought me up here?'

'I'm going to show you.'

The two women walked hand in hand up the side of the field. The girl's path was no longer to be seen but they followed the route it had taken. Halfway up the field, they stopped and the girl said, 'Here. Just here.'

They knelt on the sharp stubble of the field and looked into the hedge. There was a tunnel that had been beaten through the bracken, a fan of dry sand and small stones spread out in front of a burrow. It could have been a warren or a den, but it wasn't.

'Can you see?' asked the girl.

The woman peered into the hole. 'I don't know what I'm looking for.'

'Offer your gift,' said the girl.

The woman had a small jug of thick, clotted cream that she tentatively held out towards the burrow. She stared into the bracken, squinting into the darkness and then her eyes grew large and she snatched a shallow breath.

'Shush,' said the girl. 'You'll scare it.'

There was movement in the burrow. Slight and delicate but something moved. There was the glint of an eye and then a face, as wrinkled as a baby's and as wizened as an oak tree.

'It's all right,' said the girl. 'It's going to be all right.' She rested her hand on her mother's shoulder. 'There's three of us again now.'

# LIFECYCLE

NEARLY DEAD Dave had a head like a hard-boiled free-range egg that had been tapped by a spoon. His mottled brown skin was speckled and smooth on the domed crown but his twinkling eyes were set in a mosaic of cracks and crevices. The last few wisps of his hair stuck out like the sparks from a Van de Graaff generator. His brain was still very much alive.

He didn't sleep a great deal. He'd discovered he didn't need to. Perhaps it was because, with so little life left to him, every moment felt precious, or perhaps, as he did almost nothing all day but sit in his chair, he really didn't need to sleep at all. Most nights he just sat up in bed and ran the film of his life in his head, at least the bits he could remember.

Boffo and Mike had made him an adjustable backrest for his bed out of a sun lounger and some two-by-four. He could set it to just the right angle. If he reclined too much the fluid built up in his lungs and he would cough and cough.

It got cold at night up here in the Highlands and it

wasn't safe to run the log burner through the night so Dave had to keep himself warm with layers and layers of clothing. His stick-thin body was padded till it resembled a Michelin man made of charity shop hoodies and thrift store knitting.

It was in the small hours that he saw the light in the sky.

They were so far from anywhere, in such a remote spot, that light pollution was practically nil. Dave liked to lie there and watch the heavens swirl past his open curtains like phosphorescence in a dark ocean.

And then one night, one of the stars didn't behave properly.

At first he thought it was the space station and then, possibly, a shooting star. Perhaps it was a meteor or an asteroid? Then it was a firework, then a weather balloon catching the first rays of tomorrow's sun. At last he decided it was a UFO and with that he pulled the blanket up around his neck and drifted off to sleep.

The next morning started much the same as any other.

None of them were big on early mornings, not Boffo nor Doctor Mike, not Jane nor Candy and definitely not Nearly Dead Dave, but once upon a time they had had a system, a routine. They would get the log burners going and throw some fresh straw down the long-drop. They might check on the solar panels, the wind turbine and the batteries. Put last night's scraps to the compost along with the ash from the fires. Morning jobs. That had all fallen by the wayside now. They had been here too long. They pretty much got up as and when; all of them that is but Dave.

Boffo was in his van, standing at the sink and waiting for the kettle to boil. Jane was sprawled on the sofa, skinning up.

'The milk's off,' said Boffo.

Jane shrugged. 'I'll take it black.'

The kettle began to whistle and Boffo turned the gas off at the bottle. The water hissed in the cold mugs. The smell of the tea was faint but rather lovely.

'It's funny,' said Jane. 'We come all the way out here to live like this and what's the one thing that we can't start the day without?'

'A cup of tea.'

'Exactly. A cup of tea. Symbol of middle England and the British Raj.'

'I like tea.'

'I know, I know. So do I but it's kind of… ironic, don't you think?'

Boffo handed her a mug. 'It's not the same black, though.'

'No. No I guess not.'

Jane balanced her tea on a pile of books by the sagging sofa and lit her joint. She dropped the lighter into a bowl that held two-dozen of them, multi-coloured like sweets in a jar. She let the smoke trail out from between her lips.

Boffo blew on his tea to cool it.

'Open the curtains,' said Jane.

Boffo twitched the thick curtains behind the sink apart like an impresario opening a show.

'Fuck me,' he said quietly. Jane frowned.

Boffo stood perfectly still. Then he squinted. Then he ran his hand through his dreadlocks, pushing them back over his shoulder and then he said, 'Fuck me,' again.

'What?' asked Jane. She was studying the roach, wondering if she'd rolled it too tight.

'I think, maybe, come and look,' said Boffo and he leaned closer to the window and rubbed at it with the heel of his hand. The glass made a shrill squeak.

'What?' Jane moaned in a whiny voice and tucked her legs further beneath her.

'Did you hear anything in the night?' asked Boffo.

'Only you farting, same as always.'

'Well something happened. Come and look.'

Jane twitched her lip but she swung her feet onto the floor and stood up. She pulled the hem of her sweatshirt down and went to stand behind Boffo.

'Fucking hell, what the shit is that?' she said quietly into his ear.

The view from Boffo and Jane's van was almost exactly the same as it always was. Right in front of them was a big pile of old pallets, a couple of oil drums and a pile of useful stuff that was sheeted over with tarpaulins. To the left they could see Mike and Candy's bus; the white and gold of the original coach paint now a background for tags and graffiti. Further away the land became scrub and rough ground where the Forestry Commission had cut it years ago. Beyond that, the regimented planting of pine grew ruler-straight and saw-tooth topped.

In the middle of the scrub and under a cold, bleached-blue sky sat the problem.

'How did that get here?'

'And more to the point, what is it?'

Between their van and the far trees was a large sphere. A large, perfectly reflective sphere, like a gigantic chromed ball-bearing or the pinball on the front of the "Tommy" album. A chromed sphere about twenty metres in diameter. A twenty-metre-diameter chromed sphere sitting on five articulated legs.

It took them a while to process the information.

It stood in the landscape, perfectly round and perfectly reflective. As if it wasn't there. As if it was the world seen through a huge droplet of water. Like reality, but distorted. As if it was trying to hide, and not doing it very well.

Jane's eyes suddenly opened wide. 'Do you think anything was in it?'

'What?' said Boffo. 'Like a creepy alien that's coming to probe you?' and he turned around pulling a face and twisting one finger up in the air.

Jane growled and pushed him hard in the chest. 'Twat. We should tell the others,' she said.

.

They knocked on the door of the bus. After a while the curtain twitched back and Mike peered at them through the condensation that clouded the inside of the glass. 'What?' He mouthed the word and they saw the yellow, snaggle of his teeth. His eyes were red and his hair a mess. He was wearing a pink Hello Kitty dressing gown with a black-and-white keffiyeh snuggled around his neck.

Boffo tugged on the door handle but it was locked or stuck.

Mike rolled his eyes and opened the bus door from the inside. 'She's asleep,' he said, as soon as the door opened. 'What time is it?'

'You need to come and see this,' said Mike, but quietly. Candy wasn't a morning person.

'What?' said Mike, yawning. He scratched at his jaw then went to scratch his balls but thought better of it.

'Visitors,' said Jane.

'Or something,' said Boffo.

'Well that's clear as mud,' he said. 'Give me a minute,' and Mike disappeared back behind the curtain.

When he appeared again he had a cap on his head and Crocs on his feet. His spindly legs were still bare, sticking out from the dressing gown like a chicken's. As the cold air hit his lungs he began to cough. A racking, hacking cough that seemed to get stuck in his chest until he slammed his palm against his sternum and hawked up a mouthful of phlegm that he sent spinning away into the bushes. His eyes had watered and he rubbed them dry before reaching for Jane's splif. The smoke made him cough again and he explored the inside of his mouth with his fingers before producing a blob of greenish grey mucus, which he examined carefully.

Boffo raised his eyebrows. 'And you're the doctor are you?'

'Never said that.'

'Well, "medical professional", then.'

'Not the same thing, is it? Where are these visitors? What do they want? And what the fuckin' shitty piss-wank hell is that?'

Doctor Mike had seen the sphere.

The three of them walked to the edge of their little commune where the deforested scrub began. The land was covered with tall grass and mounds of brambles, the stumps of the trees that were cut and the saplings that had been planted to replace them. There were clumps of yellow ragwort and sprays of creamy white cow parsley, purple heather and drifts of rust-red bracken. What there wasn't was any sign of a trail or track through the scrub. Nothing had flattened any of the vegetation. Nothing had knocked over any of the saplings.

'It landed, then,' said Jane.

'I guess.'

'Looks that way.'

'It's a weather balloon,' said Mike suddenly and rather too loud.

The other two looked at him. 'No, it isn't,' said Jane,

'It quite clearly isn't.' said Boffo. 'The legs, man. It's on legs. Balloons don't have legs.'

'They don't do that, either,' said Mike and pointed at the underside of the sphere. A line had appeared in the chrome that became a crease that became a gap that defined a hatch that swung down from the body of the thing. A rectangular platform supported by a silvery mesh tube that slowly lowered itself towards the earth. Standing on the platform was a man.

'It's just some guy,' said Boffo.

'Some totally bald, naked guy?' said Jane squinting at the figure.

'Yeah,' said Doctor Mike. 'Seems it is.'

.

They let the figure come to them. Partly because they were aware of the potential dangers inherent in approaching what may prove to be an alien spacecraft but mostly because they knew better than to try and walk through the bramble and the gorse barelegged.

The closer the figure got, the clearer it became that

although it looked human, it wasn't human.

It was too perfect. The figure had the physique of an Olympic swimmer, the features of a Greek god and was as well endowed as a porn star.

It didn't seem to mind striding through the brambles and the gorse barelegged, indeed bare-everythinged.

Its features were utterly expressionless. It didn't seem to be breathing and its perfect skin was blemish-free and slightly shiny. When it was only a few yards away, they could see that its eyeballs were the same pink colour as its skin and that was really freaky.

'That's really freaky,' said Jane sharing her attention between its face and its groin.

Boffo leaned forward, peering into its face as if to detect signs of life. Mike pulled a sour expression. 'It isn't breathing, man. That ain't right.'

The alien's head turned to look at Mike. It leaned forwards, just a fraction. With a faint pop its mouth opened. Then it took a breath. Its chest rose and then fell. Then nothing. Then it breathed in again. It seemed to settle down to a normal rhythm.

'Fuck. Me,' said Mike. 'And that really isn't normal.'

'Oh right,' said Boffo. 'Like, in your experience of these things.'

'Chill, man,' said Mike frowning.

The alien took a step forward but stopped when the three of them started to shift uncomfortably away from it. Smoothly, the alien moved its head like a scanner taking in each of the people in front of it. Looking them up and down in a movement that was robotic. It looked like a body-popper warming up before the music started. Then it looked into each of their faces. It blinked, and when its eyes opened again, its eyeballs were white with coloured irises and black pupils; one eye blue and one eye green.

'Wow, man. Did you see that?' said Boffo. Mike nodded his head and grunted.

The alien opened its mouth and croaked, a coarse gravelly sound that became a low hiss.

'OK,' said Mike slowly. He frowned at the alien. 'Can you talk?' He mimicked its croaking sound. 'Can you speak,' he said.

'What are you on about, man?' said Boffo. 'What are you doing?'

'I don't know? Getting it to talk maybe. I think it's reacting to us. Like it's copying us, or something. Like machine learning. You know, the thing with the eyes and the way it started breathing?'

Boffo sighed and ran his fingers through his dreads. Mike scratched at the stubble on his chin.

'Hair,' said the alien in a raspy, scratchy voice. 'Should I have hair?' and it ran its hand over its bald pate and smooth groin.

'Christ,' said Jane. 'That does it.' She turned on her heel and walked back towards the bus and the caravans.

·

Nearly Dead Dave watched Jane stomp across the field and head towards Mike and Candy's bus.

'Something's got her chakras in a twist,' he muttered to himself.

Dave swung his legs out of bed and slowly put his feet on the floor. Carefully, he stood up and walked over to the window. If he rested his head on the glass and looked over to the right he could see Boffo and Mike talking to a naked stranger and, behind them, a massive chromed sphere on legs standing in the scrubland. 'OK,' he said to himself. His head bobbed up and down. 'OK. That explains last night sure enough.'

.

When Jane emerged from Mike and Candy's bus she was carrying a pair of shorts. Candy was following her. 'Hold up. Hold up,' said Candy, trying to keep pace with Jane. 'No rush, surely.'

'You're obscene,' said Jane.

'Oh, come on! I just want a look.'

'We are visited by an alien. This might be first contact. The first proof that we aren't alone in the universe. We, I mean like the four of us…'

'Five of us.'

'What? Yeah, I mean the five of us get to greet the first alien life form mankind has ever met and your reaction is like, "can I see his big cock?" You are so out of tune with the universe'

'You mentioned it.'

'Yes, I did, but only to explain why I wanted to borrow a pair of Mike's shorts. He'd never fit in Boffo's.' Jane skidded to a halt and turned to glower at Candy. 'By that I mean that Boffo is very slim and the alien and Mike share a more similar waist measurement. OK?'

Candy was famous for her sense of humour but this didn't look like the time or the place. 'Yeah. Fine. OK,' she said and then she tried to peer around Jane's shoulder to get a glimpse of the appendage in question.

Boffo waved at the two women. 'Come and say, hello,' he called.

Jane stomped over with Candy fluttering behind her. She pushed past the men and held the shorts out towards the alien like a matador showing the cape to the bull. 'Put these on,' she said. 'Just put them on.'

The alien gave her a quizzical look. 'Are they a gift?' it said, its voice smoother and richer now.

'Blimey. I see what you mean,' said Candy, her hand up to her mouth and eyes wide.

The alien took the shorts and held them out in front of it, studying them from every angle. 'They are a gift for...?' and it narrowed its eyes in question.

'For wearing,' said Jane and mimed stepping into a pair of shorts and doing them up.

'I'll show him,' said Candy stepping forward but Jane glowered at her. 'You show him,' she said to Boffo. Then she looked at her watch. 'It's gone ten,' she said. 'Has anyone checked on Dave? I didn't think so. Are you doing that, Mike? Come on, and let's get him out of sight,' and she nodded at the alien.

'Away from all the visitors we're always getting up here, yeah?' said Mike.

'A visitor,' said the alien. It tapped its chest and smiled at them all. 'Yes, I am a visitor.'

'Have you seen how quickly his hair is growing,' said Doctor Mike.

'I certainly have,' said Candy as the alien stepped into the shorts and pulled them up.

·

'Has he said why he's here?' asked Nearly Dead Dave as Doctor Mike fussed around him.

'Hang on. Let me check this first,' and Mike slipped a fingertip oximeter on to Dave's right hand. It flashed for a second or two then the display showed a number; eighty-six. 'Hmm, that's not great,' said Mike.

'Oh, screw that,' said Dave. 'I think I'll live long enough to meet my first alien, that's if we get on with it, eh.'

Mike chuckled. 'Let me take your pulse,' he said.

Dave held out his wrist. 'OK, but why? I mean, I am…'

'Nearly dead,' they both said in chorus and laughed.

'It's what I do, man,' said Mike. 'I took an oath to care for…'

'Mike,' said Dave. 'You dropped out of nurses training at the end of your second year. I appreciate you looking after me and all that but you aren't Doctor Kildare, you know? We've been through this, I'm dying soon, and that's it.'

Doctor Mike held Dave's hand in his; he stroked the upturned wrist with two fingers. He sighed. 'I just wish I could fix you, man.'

'I'm old. You can't fix old.'

Mike rubbed at his chin. 'I know. I know. Perhaps we should just recycle you then?' and he laughed.

'Perhaps you should,' said Nearly Dead Dave. 'So, why is he here?'

'What, the alien? I don't know. It's not really the first thing you ask, is it? What the fuck are you doing here? Seems… disrespectful.'

Dave grunted as Mike helped him on with his boots. 'Well, no one invited him, that's for sure. Help me with my coat and let's go and have a look.'

'I was on the inbound run, back to the iNode and, I know it's not what you should do but I thought I'd just cut the corner around your star but I clipped the edge of a dust cloud and holed the module so the procedure was to land as soon as possible. Which is annoying because interstellar flight is still, statistically, the safest way to travel, but here I am.'

The alien was sitting in Mike's big armchair. It had the shorts on and a crochet blanket wrapped around its shoulders. It hadn't said it was cold but it looked better covered up. More human. Less weird. It had quite a head of hair now too.

Candy was sitting by the log burner pushing sticks into the weak flames, nursing the fire back to life. Boffo and Jane sat next to each other on a sofa-bed that was about to collapse into being little more than a pile of cushions.

'Scary, man,' said Boffo.

The alien looked at him with its head on one side, as if wondering how much experience of intergalactic travel and its associated perils this man actually had. Jane was nodding, sagely. Candy lit a joint from the glowing end of a stick and tapped her ash onto the floor.

'I can repair the module. I've downloaded a couple of How2 vids and the module carries some spares. There's a patch-up nanobotics system running so it's pretty much out there fixing itself now. No offence, but I really don't want to hang around here for long.'

'Right. Right,' said Boffo. Candy rolled her eyes.

The alien suddenly took a breath and Boffo realised that it hadn't been breathing for a while, as if it had forgotten to.

'Where are you from?' asked Boffo.

'Can't explain. Very far away.'

'Do you come in peace?' asked Jane.

'I came by accident,' said the alien, looking puzzled.

'Why here? Why us?' asked Candy.

'I didn't expect to find you here. I didn't expect to find anyone here. No lights. No electronic signatures. Not even a heat signature as far as I could see. This is nowhere and you are in the middle of it.'

'How long will it take to fix your ship, man?' asked Boffo.

'I am not a man, and as I said, not long.'

Candy smiled at the alien, the fire glow warming her face. 'You look like a man,' she said. 'Well, a lot like a man.'

'This is not how I look,' said the alien. 'This...' it touched its chest, face and legs. 'This shell is bio-engineered by the module, for my survival. Rather than put my actual body into a spacesuit that can withstand this environment, the module puts my consciousness into a body that can survive here. Clever, isn't it?'

'We won't hurt you,' said Boffo.

'No,' said the alien. 'You won't.'

.

Mike held his elbow out so that Dave had something to hang on to as they stepped out of the caravan. Dave's caravan, his home, had lost its mobility some time ago and was becalmed in a sea of decking. The two men stood on it looking out at the alien sphere; shiny, pristine and somehow rather new looking.

'I know he's a space man and all that,' said Dave. 'But it does rather feel like some rich bloke has just driven up and parked in our front yard.'

Mike grunted and nodded his head. 'I'm sure he's OK. I mean, he must be pretty advanced.'

Dave turned to look at Doctor Mike. 'Mike,' he said. 'If you remember, what most of society calls "advanced" is what we're here to get away from.'

.

'Why are you here?' asked the alien.

'Oh, my god, if only we knew the answer to that question. If we knew why we were here, what our purpose is, what we are meant to become, eh? How amazing it would be if we knew that answer,' said Jane in a gush of words and smoke coiling out from her mouth. She leant towards the alien. 'We should all be seekers of truth, don't you think? Why are we here?' Her eyes sparkled with the comfort of a familiar question. 'Why. Are. We. Here?' She sighed.

'No,' said the alien. 'I meant, "Why are you people here?" Why are you living out here…with nothing… surrounded by rubbish?' The alien twitched, then it blinked twice.

Jane looked affronted. 'What?' she squeaked. 'What did you say?'

'Well,' said the alien gesturing around the bus. 'This is all pretty basic, isn't it? According to my scan your world has nuclear power and some rudimentary computing and AI. I think you've even been off-planet a few times so why are you all here and living in the Stone Age?'

'That is the most ignorant and insulting…'

'Whoa,' said Boffo, holding his palm up to Jane. 'Let's not get carried away. It's probably just a misunderstanding.' He smiled at the alien. 'This is the future, man. This is how we'll all be living. Recycling everything and growing our own food and using sustainable energy and all that.'

'Well I pretty much come from the future,' said the alien. 'And I have to say, no, it isn't.'

Boffo leant forward, the light of conviction in his eyes. 'It is, man,' he said. 'We are here because of Dave. We call him "Nearly Dead Dave" but that's because…'

'Just tell him,' said Candy.

'OK. This guy, Dave Govan was like this amazing guru in the seventies and he saw that the western world was fucked and that we couldn't keep on living the way we were and he was like well ahead of his time and believed in Gaia, the Earth spirit, and not polluting our planet and living in harmony with nature and everything.'

'He had a beautiful commune, out by the coast,' said Jane 'Like Findhorn, but not as big.'

'But that fell to pieces,' said Candy. 'Some people just weren't very cool. We met him as it was breaking up.'

'And we came out here with him,' said Boffo. 'To, like, start it all again. But he's kind of really old and…'

'Well, that's interesting,' said the alien, looking bored. He looked out at the sun slowly moving through the afternoon sky. 'By the end of this cycle I should be on my way and I can leave you to…um, all this.'

The alien blinked twice then became still. After a moment it took a piece of the crochet blanket in its fingers and began to study it as if it were a twist of DNA and the secrets of all life could be found within it.

Mike and Dave took a long time to get to the spaceship.

When they came close they saw that the mirrored surface of the sphere reflected its surroundings and made them into a huge globe; a toy planet twenty meters across. The reflected sky became a cold blue sea and the reflections of trees and bracken became land, islands and continents in green and brown.

'It's beautiful,' said Mike, quietly.

'What you're seeing is the Earth,' said Dave. 'It's the Earth that's beautiful. I have no idea what that thing is'

When they got really close their own faces, as bulbous and swollen as fleshy gargoyles, peered back at them from the globe's surface.

'What's over there?' said Dave nodding at the ground on the far side of the sphere. Mike shrugged and shook his head. 'Dunno.'

They walked around the legs; neither of them felt comfortable being underneath the vast sphere, and on the other side they came to a disturbing sight. Another hatch had opened in the structure and a platform swung out from it. There were crates and boxes, blister packs and sheets of silver mesh strewn everywhere. A corrugated tube hung down from the hatch and had disgorged a lake of brownish yellow slime that had an oily, bubbling film floating on the surface. One of the sheets of silver gauze was tangled in a thicket of brambles; another piece had been caught by the breeze and was flapping gently in the branches of a distant tree.

The two men stood in absolute silence, Dave's hand resting on Mike's elbow. Mike chewed pensively at his lip.

Dave's jaw set hard in anger.

'Oh,' said Mike eventually.

'Yeah,' said Dave. 'Oh.'

Another sheet of mesh tumbled down from the platform and blew across the scrubland until it snagged in on a sapling. Mike took a step forward but Dave pulled him back.

'Leave it,' he said. 'Where is this spaceman?'

Mike nodded towards his bus.

Dave took a deep sigh. 'Let's say hello, shall we?' and with Mike supporting him, they began to walk back towards the camp.

.

'You aren't you, are you?' said Candy, still feeding the fire.

The alien smiled. 'No. This body is a construct. My consciousness is in the module. This is how we hide and survive on raw worlds. We copy the dominant species.' Candy nodded. The alien held up its hand and turned it in the light. 'You would call this body a drone, perhaps a clone. Not a robot. It's much more than you would mean by that. It isn't alive, but it has my life within it. It's a piece of single-use bio-tech.'

'Raw worlds?' asked Candy.

'Ones that...' The alien seemed to think for a second. 'One's that still believe they are alone. Raw. Yes, raw worlds.'

'Shit,' said Boffo. The alien smiled at him and nodded.

'Are you amazingly advanced?' asked Jane. 'Are you, like, a superior being?'

The alien glanced at it's module, gleaming in the

radiation of the nearest star then it looked at the log burner and the collapsed sofa and the battered laptop that sat on top of the table and the digital radio that was tuned to Radio6.

'Yes,' it said. 'I believe so.'

The door to the bus swung open and Doctor Mike stepped inside.

'I think Dave wants a word with the spaceman,' he said.

'I prefer to identify as "alien" rather then "space man",' said the alien.

'Right,' said Mike. 'Right. Anyway…' and he turned and helped Dave climb through the door.

Nearly Dead Dave had never looked so appropriately named. He was pale and shaking. His right hand twitched in a spastic dance. With his left hand he held tight to Mike's elbow. His head appeared to be heavy on his neck and his neck seemed weak but his eyes shone and his mouth was still set in a tight line.

He climbed the two steps into the bus and fixed his eyes on the alien.

'Get off…' he began but then had to take a breath. 'Get off my…' He stopped and coughed and began again. 'Get off my land,' he said at last. 'In fact, get off my fucking planet,' he snarled at the alien.

'Hey, man,' said Boffo. 'What the fuck?'

'Get this creature out of my sight. Get this filthy, polluting specimen off my land.'

'Not a "spacemen",' said the alien. 'I'm an…'

'I said "specimen" you idiot,' said Dave and then he slowly let himself collapse into a wooden chair by the table. His body sagged on to his arse and his elbows but his eyes were still fixed on the alien.

'I'm sure he thinks he's "superior" and "advanced" and "the future" but I've heard shit like that my entire life. I heard it about nuclear power and I heard it about fracking. I heard people deny climate change and tell us that plastic and oil and carbon weren't the problem. Well, I've had enough of it. He's been here for ten minutes, on a planet that isn't even his, for Christ's sake, and he's polluted our environment. He's strewn his rubbish all over it. His spaceship is probably nuclear powered and it's parked just out there.'

'Nuclear!' said the alien. 'I wouldn't fly anything out of a museum, would I? Nuclear powered? Hardly, it uses and infusion proton drive that…'

'Go,' said Dave, although he sounded nearly dead.

"What's the problem here?' said the alien. 'I had a tidy-out, dumped some stuff. The coolant needed draining so there's that, and I had to un-box a few spare parts for the repairs. What's it matter? Who cares about a bit of rubbish? What difference does it make?'

Doctor Mike was standing behind Dave and he started to shake his head in disbelief. Candy let her head drop to one side as she glared at the alien. Boffo and Jane snuggled closer to each other on the sofa, scowls on both their faces.

'Did you?' asked Candy.

'What?'

'Pollute our planet.'

'So what?'

'That's just so wrong,' said Candy.

The alien twitched and then blinked twice. Three times. It twitched again and then sat absolutely still.

'Can you help me back to my van, please,' said Dave very quietly. His breathing was shallow and rapid. He kept licking his lips; they were dark red against the pallor of his skin.

.

While Mike helped Dave back to his van the others took a walk out to the sphere. They left the alien sitting in the bus. When they could see the rubbish that had come from the alien's ship spread across the landscape they stopped. Boffo took Jane's hand and squeezed it. Candy put her hand up to her face and covered her mouth. They stood like that for a little while.

'My mum used to have this doormat,' said Candy almost to herself. 'It had a little picture of a spaceman on it and it said "Aliens welcome". It was a bit of fun, but mum sort of meant it as well.'

Boffo and Jane turned to look at her.

'I grew up in a house that not only believed in aliens but also really, really wanted them to turn up. Spock and Star Trek. Mork and Mindy. Aliens were better than us and they would help us. They'd show us what to do. They would save the day. It was just what I believed. I think we all did.'

Boffo nodded. 'Yeah,' he muttered. 'I know. Me too.'

'And I just don't know what she'd say. I really don't.'

'Your mum?'

'Yeah. My mum.'

A transparent blister pack fell off the platform, the wind caught it and it tumbled across the ground before getting stuck in the pool of oily slime.

'I think she'd be angry, and I think she'd be sad too.'

'What are we going to do?' asked Jane.

'What are we going to do?' asked Mike, jogging up to them from the direction of Dave's caravan. 'Dave's not looking so good. I put him in his chair and gave him some oxygen.' He stopped and looked at the rubbish strewn everywhere. 'And what're we going to do about this?'

Boffo shook his head and shrugged. Candy looked down at the ground.

'We're going to clear it up,' said Jane. 'What else?'

They talked it over for a little while but eventually it came to seem like the only thing they could do. Boffo went back to the vans and returned with a pile of black bin bags. He brought gloves and an extendable grab that had once been used for picking apples.

'For that stuff in the trees over there,' he'd explained when Mike had looked quizzically at it.

They took a bag each and began to collect everything that had spilled from the alien's module. Most of it seemed to be packaging and packing and made of stuff that was either similar to plastic or a bit like metal. Most of the metal seemed to be too light and most of the plastic felt soft or even sticky.

'Shall we keep the materials separate?' asked Boffo.

'You do realise we won't be taking this to the recycling centre, don't you?' said Candy and Boffo grunted in embarrassment.

'What about that?' asked Mike looking at the pool of slime.

.

The alien twitched and then it blinked twice.

It stood up and the crochet blanket slipped to the floor.

It bent to pick it up but then stopped and focussed on the wooden boards that made up the floor of the bus. When it did stand, it turned to look at the MDF kitchen units and sink that had been squeezed under the bus's window. It looked at the chimney of the log burner that disappeared up through the ceiling. It looked at two bins beneath the sink, one marked "glass" and the other "plastic'. It looked inside them. It looked at the wooden stairs and bannister that ran up to the sleeping platform at the back of the bus and it looked at the driving seat and steering wheel that was still at the front.

The alien blinked.

There was movement outside the window and the alien turned and watched Candy stomp past the wheelie bins and then pull the tarpaulin off a big pile of what looked like rubbish. She pulled a drum out from the pile and then, after a bit of digging and ferreting, she produced a bucket. The alien watched her replace the tarpaulin. She lashed it back down again before picking up the drum and bucket and heading back to the module.

The alien blinked. It stepped out through the bus door and followed her.

Candy marched through the site, the drum banging against her thigh with each and every angry step. The alien kept up with her, unconcerned as to whether its bare feet were coming down on mud or stone, nettle or grass.

They crossed the scrubland and went round to the other side of the sphere. Most of the rubbish had been collected and Boffo was putting all the bin bags into a pile.

'We're almost done,' called Jane.

'Almost,' and she walked up to the oily pool. She put the drum down and then went to scoop the bucket into the thick liquid.

'No!' shouted the alien. 'Do not... Do not touch it. Step away.'

'What?' said Candy. She frowned. 'Why?'

'There may be some risk...' said the alien. 'It is probably better if you don't touch...'

'Oh. Is it dangerous?'

'A biological organism like yourself might...'

'Is it dangerous to life? Is it dangerous to my life?'

'There are compounds in it that might affect...'

'You knew this was poisonous. You knew this was toxic and you dumped it anyway?'

'It will soak away into the substrate. It will be absorbed by...'

'Oh, not to fucking worry then because it will just soak into the earth, whatever the fuck it is. Just don't touch it first in case you die. Is that what you're saying because that is what it fuckin' sounds like.'

The alien walked up to Candy and held his hand out for the bucket.

'I didn't expect you to...'

'Didn't expect us to clean up our own planet? No, well,' said Candy. 'I can't say you are alone in that.'

.

Within the hour the alien had pumped the effluent back into the module along with any ground that might have soaked it up. The bags of rubbish had been loaded back on to the platform and were now inside the ship.

'Why couldn't you have done that in the first place?' asked Candy.

'Saving weight,' said the alien. 'Less weight. Less fuel. Less cost,'

'Christ,' said Boffo. 'Welcome to the future.'

'Well done, anyway,' said Jane. 'Doesn't your aura feel brighter now? It certainly looks it,' and she hugged one of it's hands in both of hers.

'Jane,' said Boffo. 'It's a fucking alien, you know.'

'All creatures have an aura,' said Jane smugly.

The alien blinked. 'I did tell you about the "single-use bio-tech" thing, didn't I? I'm sure I did.'

'Is your space ship thingy fixed?' asked Boffo pointing to the sphere.

'Yes. It's time I was…'

An alarm went off over by the vans and, at the same time, the mobile in Mike's pocket started to squawk. The alien's head whipped around scanning the horizon, left to right and then back again.

'No, chill,' said Mike. 'It's Dave. His alarm's gone off.' Mike's face crumpled. 'Oh god, his alarm's gone off.'

The four humans ran towards Dave's caravan with the alien following them. They reached the decking outside Dave's caravan in a confused squabble of arms and legs, like a bucket load of people being spilled onto the ground. The alien held back. Doctor Mike was first through the door.

Dave was sitting in his comfy chair, slumped back against the cushions. He looked deflated. On the index finger of his right hand the oximeter was wired to an old NHS monitor that was bleeping and flashing and had triggered the alarm.

Mike peered at the numbers flicking slowly downwards and the heart monitor line that drew a picture of Dave's every breath and heartbeat. 'Oh, no man,' whispered Mike. 'Not here. Not now.'

Dave's eyes were half closed. His eyelids fluttered like leaves in autumn. His skin was paler, his lips darker. He was breathing but his chest hardly rose and fell at all.

'What is happening?' asked the alien.

'He's dying.'

'Then stop it. Stop it happening.'

'We can't. I can't.'

But Dave could. His eyes opened wide and he took a long, long breath in. His chest actually began to rise. His berry-red lips parted and he sucked air in through his mouth. His nostrils flared.

'Not... yet,' he gasped and smiled at the faces around him. 'I thought I was a goner there. I thought that was... me done.' His eyes watered and he blinked the tears away. There was the faintest smile on his lips. 'Nearly dead isn't dead though, is it?'

The line on the monitor seemed to agree with him and the blood oxygen level clicked up a digit or two.

Boffo, Mike, Jane and Candy patted his hand, pushed some of the wisps of his hair into place, put a hand on his shoulder as if physical contact reassured them that he was still with them.

'Enough,' said Mike at last. 'Enough. Give him some air.'

'Why are you dying?' asked the alien.

'Because... because I'm old,' said Dave. 'This body is old. It's worn out.'

'Your mind is still alive. Your mind is strong.'

Dave shrugged. 'You kind of need a body to keep your mind in though. Anyway, we all die. Everyone dies.'

The alien blinked.

'I shall be leaving soon,' it said.

'Good,' said Dave.

'The jetsam, the ejecta, the rubbish, it's all gone. It is back in the module. I will take it with me.'

'And dump it where?' said Dave. 'Someone else's planet?'

The alien blinked. 'You would care about that just as much as if it was here, wouldn't you?'

'Yes,' said Dave. 'Of course. How can anyone not.'

'What should I do with it?'

'Can it be recycled?' asked Dave.

'What is "recycled"?'

Dave took a shallow breath. He moistened his lips. He flapped his free hand at his four friends. 'Off you go. I'll be fine,' and then he looked at the alien. 'You better come and sit down. This might take a while.'

.

'Funny old day,' said Boffo as he rolled a spliff and waited for his tea to cool.

'Just a bit,' said Mike. 'Your mum would be happy for you, eh?' he said to Candy. 'You know, that you'd met an alien. I wonder what they are talking about?'

'It's talking to Dave,' said Boffo. 'I think we know what they are talking about. It's what he's been talking about for the last forty years.'

'I was scared.'

'Eh?'

'I was scared when Dave's alarm went off. He's not got much longer, has he?' said Jane. 'Has he?'

No one said anything. Boffo blew on his tea and looked

blankly out of the window. Candy stared at the fire sprites dancing on top of the ash-grey logs. Mike and Jane looked into each other's eyes trying to measure the amount of sadness the other was feeling.

'No,' said Doctor Mike. 'He's not got long.'

'What's actually wrong with him?'

'He's just about to break. He's worn out. He'll break like a car. You know how it goes; the hoses start to leak and the pipes get furred up. The pump stops working and the chassis starts to creak and bits fall off. One morning it just won't start or perhaps it stops dead on the way to the shops and leaves you stranded by the side of the road. No reason, really. Just old and worn out and, I guess, it's time has come.'

'Oh, nice' said Jane dripping sarcasm on to the floor.

'Just telling it how it is, babe. I'm sorry.'

'I think you might have got it wrong though,' said Boffo. 'Look out there,' and he pointed through the window to where the alien was carrying Nearly Dead Dave towards the sphere. The alien's forearms were stuck out like the prongs on a forklift truck and Dave was lying across them, one arm hooked around its neck. The crochet blanket had been lost somewhere along the way. The alien was walking slowly and steadily, his pink and perfect nearly naked body in stark contrast to the bundle of rags that was Dave. Even at this distance they could see Dave's lips were moving.

'What the fuck is going on,' said Boffo.

'They are talking,' said Jane. 'I can see his lips.'

'He's not struggling,' said Candy.

Mike leapt up and made for the door. He burst through it and, shouting Dave's name, ran towards the two figures with the others following behind. They had only got to the edge of the scrub when the alien reached the platform that had descended from the sphere when he had first arrived. He stepped on to it and, like a lift, it began to rise carrying the pair of them up into the module.

Mike and the others realised that they wouldn't get there in time and so they simply stopped. Like marionettes with cut strings or battery-operated toys gone flat they came to a halt and stood blank and motionless watching the lift disappear into the ship.

'Body snatcher!' shouted Boffo and Mike frowned at him out of the corner of his eye. Jane started crying.

The sun dropped to below the treeline. The ball of burning plasma set the trees alight even from one hundred and fifty million kilometres away. Where the light touched the black silhouettes they burst into orange, yellow and red; the light was so intense it burnt their visible shapes away to nothing and that life-giving ball set the sky to glowing red. The alien's reflecting sphere became a droplet of blood caught and frozen just before it fell to earth.

And then the hatch in the base of the sphere opened once again.

The platform descended.

The alien still carried Dave but this time Dave was clearly dead.

Jane fell to her knees, sobbing. Mike hunched his shoulders and bit his thumb. Candy and Boffo put their arms around the other two.

'We need to bury this,' said the alien holding out Dave's body.

'It's not a thing you monster. That's our friend.'

'No,' said the alien. 'It isn't.'

The alien moved slightly, it appeared to tentatively offer

the body out towards Mike. 'You take it mate,' it said. 'You've looked after it for so long,' and it sighed. A deep and very human sigh.

Mike frowned and peered closer at the alien's face.

'Come again,' he said.

'You looked after this body for such a long time. You kept it going. You kept me going. Thank you.' The alien bit its lip; chewed at the flesh.

Mike reached out and touched the side of the alien's face, a delicate hand on its cheek feeling for the bones beneath the skin.

Mike blinked. 'What did you call this thing,' he said. 'A "single-use bio-tech" or something, wasn't it?'

A huge grin lit up the alien's face. 'You worked it out,' it said. 'You worked it out.' The eyes in that perfectly handsome face twinkled with an intensity that Mike recognised.

'Dave?' he asked. 'Is it you?'

'I explained it all to him. Re-cycling. Up-cycling. Extending the useful life of something…'

'And he got it?'

'Yeah. He got it.'

'So he put your… soul? Conscience? Mind?'

'Whatever,' said Dave from inside the alien.

'He put you into the body he'd been using.'

The alien shape nodded down at Totally Dead Dave in his arms. 'Yeah. That's why I don't need this anymore,' and he smiled, just the way he used to smile back in the old days.

'Awesome,' muttered Boffo, pulling the twisted remains of a spliff out of one pocket and a sherbet-coloured lighter from the other.

# THE HEDGEROWS AND
# THE AISLES

I STARTED going for walks in that long, glorious and dreadful spring.

I had never been much for walking before. Shanks's pony had always seemed to me like a poor form of transport, a dull form of entertainment and a feeble excuse for exercise. That view might also have been coloured by the fact that I now had old knees. No older than any of the rest of me, I grant you, but old and rather creaky all the same.

Sometimes it felt as if getting older was the process of turning back into a caterpillar after you had spent decades being a butterfly. I no longer floated through the world but rather I made slow and careful progress along my branch of life wondering when I might fall off.

Of course, just when you think you have your life mapped out nicely for the foreseeable future, up to the next bend in the road at least, that's when the world changes and shreds all your plans.

It shouldn't have come as any surprise and in some ways it didn't. We had all been telling each other stories about the end of the world for as long as I can remember, but communists with atom bombs had been supplanted by terrorists with home-made explosives; starvation and famine had been replaced with the threat of worldwide obesity; and now we all squabbled over whether global warming was more or less disastrous than an impending oil crisis.

We were all looking the wrong way.

As any deluge begins with one raindrop, this all began with one death. But the cloudburst wasn't far behind. The busy and industrious world that we had built turned out to be fragile and delicate. Pestilence didn't spread across the world riding a pale horse; rather it travelled by 737 and Airbus. It arrived more quickly that way. Pestilence walked through arrivals with a mild temperature and a duty-free bottle of whisky.

For my part, my first walk was still weeks away and the hedgerows were still brown.

For decades we had been exhorting each other to Save the Planet or at the very least paying lip service to the phrase. Within a few weeks of the pale horseman's arrival by air, we were being told to Save Lives. Presumably the high panjandrums had realised that in this instance the planet could look after herself. Overpopulation and overcrowding had long been the bugbears of the troubled classes and now people were killing other people simply by standing too close to them. If it weren't so dreadful, it would be ironic; nature has a well-developed sense of irony.

I think it's important to remember that one of the first reactions, once we realised the seriousness of the situation, was: this is not the apocalypse we were looking for. There were no zombies. Life refused to stick to the clear and logical narrative arc of 'Contagion'. There were no monkeys – as far as we knew - and no Bruce Willis. We were confused. We had told ourselves the story of this moment in any number of books and films and the horror that we found ourselves living through was far more parochial and pedestrian, and all the more dreadful for that. Yes, it's true to say that for a time Famine rode his black horse through the land but when the dust cleared, we saw that mostly what he had blighted was supplies of toilet paper, strong flour and yeast. Even now, as I lace up my walking shoes and find my stick, I can remember that the thought of empty supermarket aisles and fighting OAPs for the last can of hotdogs was what frightened me most.

I was wrong.

The most dreadful thing was not a shortage of baked beans but a shortage of people and we weren't to realise that for some time to come.

I wonder how many people prayed?

The four horsemen had been a biblical apocalypse but this airline-borne pestilence was a scientific one. No priests or monks offered dispensations. No incense or holy water anointed the diseased. We turned to science and followed her blindly. The professor spoke to his congregation from behind a lectern and in front of a camera. Our icons became the graph and the chart. Our incantations were soundbites penned by spin-doctors. We lived in a post-belief world and that was the truth. We'll follow the science, they chanted. We will be led by the science, was our response.

So at first we watched the numbers rise while we washed our hands a bit more often than we normally did and we went to the pub or sat in a restaurant and made jokes about herd immunity. Then one of the scientists ran the numbers again and they must have thought that they simply had the decimal point in the wrong place but it turned out that they didn't and within a day or two the world was a very different place.

All the people disappeared.

Even now it's difficult to remember what those first few days of lockdown felt like. The shock was almost visceral. This was the apocalypse we had been looking for. These deserted streets and empty cities were the images we had been expecting. Through locations like these we could walk with Will Smith and Charlton Heston. Now, for the first time, the reality was living up to the story.

We went from that twenty-first century scrabble to cram as much as possible into every waking moment to a full stop in no time.

Overnight.

Instantly.

No wonder so many of us were damaged.

From being exhorted to do everything and buy everything we crash-stopped to the exact opposite. Do nothing and do it in your own home, alone.

I spent my days staring into the crystal ball of my computer waiting for the riots and the insurrection and the mobs. I'd seen the movie often enough so I knew what happened at the beginning of the second act but it resolutely failed to materialise. I listened to the mainstream news until the lack of stories about looting drove me to search further afield for a truth that I was convinced was happening but going unreported.

Once again, I was wrong.

It seems that Hollywood has a lower opinion of us than we have of ourselves. Hordes of rioters failed to throng our streets. Inner-city youth was too busy picking up their

Nan's prescription and a loaf of bread to go looting. There were exceptions of course. Middle-aged white woman fought like hellcats over multipacks of toilet tissue but no one knew why.

And the statistics, reported each evening, continued to tick over like the milometer of an old car being driven off a cliff; each digit another death.

And the statistics were all we had.

The only narrative was the numbers. A pandemic is an exercise in maths, someone had said, but that didn't add up. A pandemic is an exercise in sickness and death and every death needs to be mourned and everyone who a death leaves behind needs to grieve but the pestilence denied us that. Too many people went from the isolation of their own homes to the separation of a hospital ward and from there, in a bag, to a morgue.

The people, who at first became invisible, disappeared. The world began to drain of human life just as sand flows through an hourglass; unstoppably, just a function of time. Those empty streets should have been choked with one funeral cortège after another; a solemn, never-ending procession that lamented every single life, but that never happened. The funeral blooms, the lilies and the orchids, withered back, uncut, into the ground. The slow black hearses stayed in their garages.

There was a road at the end of my drive that was busy enough under most circumstances but which had fallen into immediate disuse. Sometimes more than an hour would go by without a car being on it. On one of those early, pre-walk days, I took my car out to explore, to see what could be seen. After driving for just a short while and seeing no one else on the road I began to fear breaking down and having to walk all the way home so I turned left where I had intended to turn right, cut my journey short and made my way home where I put the car away and where it has been ever since.

We were all locked in solitary.

Lockdown, a prison word for a prison thing. Inmates are separated and keys are turned. Our food was effectively rationed and many of us stood in line for it, although I was fortunate enough to have food parcels dropped by a white van. We were told that we could enjoy just an hour of exercise a day. We didn't seem to notice these subtle cultural references to a state of incarceration, or perhaps we did but just didn't care.

Of course, we weren't alone in our confinement. Before long the sun never set on people who were forced to live indoors. The countries that the pestilence had infected covered every time zone across the world. Rather foolishly I joined the chatter about the contagion being a great leveller, how it affected us all without fear or favour. Utter nonsense. Read the stories from Cape Flats or Mumbai. Watch the videos from the North American ghettos or the migrant worker dormitories in Saudi. As someone said, being in lockdown is a privilege; it shows you have a roof and four walls. Only those who have the space can practice social distancing.

I rattled around my old farmhouse like a stone in a shoe.

I didn't just have a front and a back garden; the house was afloat in a sea of lawns and borders.

It took me five minutes to walk to the top corner of my furthest field.

I learned to keep my Facebook posts quiet on the

subject of equal suffering and shared experience.

And all this time, the weather continued to be glorious.

I've always liked the idea of the pathetic fallacy. Nature should reflect our moods; the weather should act as a barometer of our feelings. But that spring seemed to take an ironic delight in being contrary to how the majority of people were feeling. Every morning was still and bright and delightful and each morning led on to a day of blues skies and a benevolently radiant sun. The weather was just perfect and it became hard to tell if Mother Nature was trying to put a balm on our hurts or if she was mocking our plight and showing just how little she damn well cared; you had your chance to save the planet, well guess what, you missed it.

Every morning I would slip out of bed and unlatch the shutters and open them to the new day. Dappled sunlight piercing the trees, A field of hay shining like a sandy beach speckled with dandelion pebbles, all under the washed-out silk of a pale-blue sky.

This was a gift but there was a price.

While my shutters were still barricaded against the daylight I would wake and remember my dreams, like smoke, like a vapour distilled from anxiety and fear. In the night I had been scared to death. Somewhere outside this old house was something that was hunting me. Somewhere out there was a ravening beast that wanted to rip my flesh and grind my bones. Something wanted to catch me and hold me, it growled and howled, clawed and pawed with a desire to rip out my throat and tear open my chest. It was huge. It was fearful. It was insubstantial. It was faint. And it terrified me for the first few moments of every day. It seemed to be like a fog, like weir lights swirling in the mist. It was a monster and it made me frightened. It was searching for me implacably. It had resolve and cruel purpose. When I woke I could feel it, just outside. I lay very still and quiet. I knew it was the virus but I knew it was an animal as well, a beast rather. It was a natural thing, an ancient predator come to cull the herd or just to feast, as it occasionally must.

On some mornings, I cried; and on some evenings as well.

And then one morning I woke and it was no longer there. No longer outside, no longer inside my head. I threw open the shutters and the day was glorious and also terrible. The world outside my window was a riot of colour and life and yet it felt as if the angel of death had passed over the place, as if the body-cart and the cries to bring out your dead had just that second turned the corner into another street, as if a man had stood at my door with a brush loaded with red paint and, after checking his list, moved on leaving the wood un-marked, the door uncrossed. I have all these memories of tumbrels and plague pits, of doctors wearing masks in the form of birds. Where are they dug up from, I wonder? At any rate, they were gone, killed by the sunlight of a perfect day.

And I thought how good it might be to take a walk.

They say that every journey starts with that first step and at first all I did was to take a walk around my garden. Actually, at first not even that. I dragged a chair outside and put it down on the lawn. Sat there with a cup of tea in my hand listening to all the little sounds that you can hear when the world has fallen silent. Leaves rustle and bees join together to make a deep rumble like ancient machinery.

I'm not much for gardening myself and of course my

regular man hadn't been for some time and so what I saw all around my chair and over the top of my tea mug was a slow wilding of the garden. Lawns saw the opportunity to become meadows. Weeds bullied their way past more carefully chosen plants and proved to be just as beautiful. The fields, like lakes, had filled up with deep, rippling grass and if I waded through them, I left a distinct wake.

As one day slipped into the next I found myself less and less likely to turn the computer on, unless I felt the urge to tinker with my shopping list. I let the news become old and I distanced myself from Facebook and all the rest.

I found a pile of books in the spare room. Some of them were so old they had pages the colour of tea but the stories in them seemed comforting and familiar even though I had forgotten I had ever owned them, let alone read them. Life slowed down to the passage of the sun through the sky and the gentle, dexterous turn of a page.

It was when I went back to the spare room to find a new book that I came across my old walking stick. A length of rough wood with a handle as smoothly polished and rounded as the ball on the top of a femur. I had bought it after some fall or other. After I got better it was just too nice to throw away. I picked it up and stabbed the ferrule at the floor a couple of times in a proprietorial manner. It felt good. It seemed like a sign.

On that first walk I took a folded up surgical mask that I put in my pocket, my mobile phone, a bottle of water, a whistle – would you believe – and my stick. There was a little gate in one of the field hedges that led out onto a path that ran along the side of the property. I let myself through it and was off my own land for the first time in goodness knows how long.

The path was a holloway, a sunken lane that had been roofed over by the trees on either side so that it became a tunnel that wound its way through the greenery. Looking along the length of the lane was like looking down into a whirlpool of greenery. The hedgerows curled up in waves that broke into a spray of gorse and hawthorn blossom. The floor of the holloway was a silky smooth, fine mud scattered with last year's dead leaves.

I stepped out, twirling the stick like a majorette.

Thin brambles hung down like vines from the branches overhead. The drone of bees pulsed like a heartbeat; they were motes of gold flowing through this artery of green, organic life. A little way ahead, two butterflies fluttered in and out of the mottled patches of light, tiny blood-red kites fighting without strings.

There were signs of other, larger life as well. Burrows and holes were let into the sandy banks. There were paths and trails that led from one side of the lane to the other where rabbits and foxes and lord knows what else regularly criss-crossed this world, unseen but leaving their sign behind.

I walked to the top of the path, a gentle slope that ended in a rusted and ramshackle stile leading in turn to a path across a softly curving hill of thistle and grass. As I emerged from the holloway and into the light a rabbit saw me, sat bolt upright and then ran for the cover of a mound of bramble, its bobbing tail flashing a danger sign to the others in the field.

And that seemed far enough. Suddenly my heart was in my throat and I could sense that ravening beast sense me. The breeze that swayed the tall grass was blowing what towards me? Pestilence? Obviously not but just the thought was enough and I tuned on my heel and walked home a little quicker than I had set out. Once I was home, I locked the door behind me without logic sense or reason, but it felt better that way.

The next morning, when I woke, I realised that I had been dreaming of that walk. In the night I had smelt the blossom and the mud, I had heard the bees and the creak of branches rubbed by the breeze. I had felt what it was to be enfolded in nature and somehow, held safe.

All the same, it was two more days before I braved the wide world once again. On this second walk, I left the whistle at home.

Once again I went out through the small gate and along the holloway to the meadow hill but this time I crossed the open field and went through a broken kissing-gate into another, larger pathway. This felt wide enough to have been a bridle path at some time but already the hedges on each side were growing in towards each other. No one was riding the path anymore and nature was reclaiming what was hers. From the top of the hill I turned and looked back over the way I had come. My old house was just visible, nestled in a stand of trees. From up here, the sky over the valley was big. A clear blue canopy that, I suddenly realised, had no contrails, no signs of air travel at all. The virus had perhaps been the last global traveller and it had already got to just about everywhere it wanted to go. It was unlikely that it had a return ticket.

I leant on my stick. My hands wrapped around its ball-joint end, fingers woven together.

There was movement in the hedge at the foot of the hill. A fox slid out into the meadow; a triangular head, flat back and bushy tail. It was as red as rust. For a moment we looked at each other and then he, or she, decided that

I wasn't worth the candle and it trotted across the field towards the bramble patch and the prospect of a rabbit dinner.

I could see half a dozen houses dotted across the valley but I couldn't tell if they were occupied or not. I could see the main road and it was empty. Some wind turbines turned on the far horizon though, which was something.

Fat horseflies and worker bees patrolled the path I walked on now. There was a rustle from the hedge as I passed and, even though I parted the bracken with my stick, I couldn't see what had caused it. I came to a crossroads and, unsure as to whether to turn left or right, I turned tail and walked back home.

The horror still continued.

I knew the pestilence was still crawling across the country but in some ways its effects were as invisible as the virus itself. The tens of thousands of dead had become too many for us to ever see. A single death is a tragedy, a million deaths is a statistic. That we should ever look to Stalin for insights into our modern lives. He spoke in a time when life was cheaper but perhaps it has somehow been devalued once again. Certainly the politicians felt themselves able to put an economic cost to the toll and decide when they had paid enough.

Days rolled by. Idyllic days. Perfect days. If only it hadn't been for all the deaths.

Like the Omega Man in a country setting, I lost myself in solitary thought and lonely pastimes. Like my garden, I felt that I was being re-wilded, going back to a nature I had fictionalised but never experienced before. I slept early, going to bed soon after supper, but then woke in the middle of the night and lay, calm and peaceful and still until second sleep came and I dozed through to the soft glow of morning. Some days I would sit cross-legged, like an African bushman, staring at the tree line across the fields, waiting for wildlife or game to appear; meditation that felt like something inherited from a hundred generations ago or more. On the kitchen counter my mobile phone lay lifeless and uncharged. I forgot to change my shopping list and the white van dropped off exactly the same supplies every few days and I ate exactly the same meals. I wore the same clothes, literally, day after day.

Rabbits sat in my garden now unconcerned about my presence. They seemed to feel the same sense of ownership and entitlement as I did. One morning I opened the shutters and saw two roe deer nibbling at the bushes. They looked my way and then finished their breakfast before dissolving into the shrubbery without a sound, almost without movement, like a fading mirage. Where the lawns had grown tall and wild, the grass showed animal tracks where a pathway had been beaten down flat by foxes or perhaps badgers or who knew what else was slowly re-colonising my little part of the world.

With each walk I roamed further and further afield.

The countryside that I walked in was like a badly folded map. There seemed to be no sense, rhyme or reason as to how the paths and lanes ran into each other, how they connected and where each one led. At first I worried about getting lost and was always careful to re-trace my steps but as time slipped by I became braver, or perhaps just more foolhardy. I found myself in new landscapes with little or no idea as to how I got there. I looked out over new views. There were woods that grew so thick and dense that once I had burrowed into them it felt as if I had to find the right tunnel – running between pit-prop trunks and supporting trees - which would lead me out in to the open air again. Every now and then I glimpsed a house in the distance or walked past one on a shady lane. They always looked closed and locked and I tried to not think of what might be inside them.

I felt as if nature was overgrowing me just as she was the countryside I walked through. My sense of smell became more acute and my hearing became sharper. I saw the world that I walked through with greater clarity. I saw a mayfly hover above a pond and I watched its wings beat. I heard a scurrying noise by the path's edge and saw the tiny movements in a blade of grass as some small creature brushed by. Looking down into a hedgerow burrow I could swear that I saw a single golden eye looking back at me.

In the world I walked through, I found peace. On the now-rare occasions that I turned to the news I found the opposite.

People died. Their deaths recorded only in indecipherable graphs and ever-growing numbers. As individuals, they simply disappeared. Dictators and despots have long known how unsettling disappearances can be. They are a nameless fear. They are lives whose story isn't told to its end. They are erased. No goodbyes. Nothing. In its shapeless, thoughtless cruelty, that is what the pestilence delivered.

For my part, I sank into my addiction with nature. I needed a stronger dose every day, I needed it earlier and I needed it to last longer.

The weather continued to be blissful and I walked in shorts and a t-shirt, sometimes even bare-chested. My stick had become an extra limb. It helped me up hills and over stiles. It was there to lean on when I needed a rest, there to

clear the bracken and brambles from my way. I lost weight.
I tanned. The pestilence certainly made me much fitter.

The landscape I walked through was like an unmade
jigsaw; this piece a field, this piece a copse, on this one
a pond fed by a stream. I had no idea what the picture
would prove to be if all the pieces were put together. I had
no idea if they even could be put together. The world was
in fragments.

I began to think that something was watching me on
my walks.

I was the intruder. I was the outlier. I was the test
case for some naturalistic singularity. I wanted to be fully
accepted; I dreamed that I would be absorbed by this new
world that was simply the old one, scrubbed clean of man's
corruption.

I became a creature of nature, alert to the smells, sights
and sounds that surrounded me and so it was no surprise
that, even over my own footfalls and my own breathing,
I heard the crack of a twig and the sound of a muffled
breath.

Like any wild creature, I froze.

The path I was on curved across the bottom of a meadow
and then led into a thicket of trees and bracken. In the
deep shadow there was a stone wall pierced by a window
and a roof of grey slate. The canopy filtered sunlight into
a kaleidoscopic pattern of bright glare. It flashed orange
reflections from the cottages window like a hazard light.
Nature had grown in here, filling the gaps. A low bough
looked like a set of antlers, a clump of bracken looked like
a russet flank.

I took a careful step forward. I felt my heart beat. I
sniffed at the still air.

Did something gleam in the shadows? Did the light catch a dark eye?

I stepped into the shade of the trees and with the sun no longer in my eyes I saw clearly and screamed. It wasn't nature that had sought me out; it was the pestilence that had found me.

The virus stood in the shadows.

It was as tall as a man but wrinkled and creased, without definition. Two legs, two arms but roughly drawn, like an amoeba, slippery and smooth. The arms ended in fingerless stumps. The feet were deformed hooves. It was faceless. Where there should have been a mouth and nose there were folds like gills. Its eyes were behind a translucent caul.

It was the virus, inhuman and strange.

I staggered and only my stick kept me upright. The ferrule dug into the earth and that solid, smooth ball nestled in my palm. I took a deep breath and hefted the stick into the air. Caught it and held it like a club, like a shillelagh. I would defend myself. I would fight back. I steeped towards the beast.

'Why aren't you wearing a mask?' it said, muffled and indistinct. 'You should be wearing a mask.' Behind the beast I now saw another figure in a Hazmat suit, exactly the same, and behind that, parked in the lane beside a cottage, an ambulance and a body in a bag on a gurney. 'Sir, you really need to be wearing a mask.'

# 얼굴을 잃는
# LOSING FACE
# OR
# THE MASK OF THE RED DEATH

LIFE IN Europe became unbearable. The virus changed things beyond all belief.

The cities became deserted and towns and villages became watchful and alert to strangers. People stayed at home, they stayed in. I could still feed but it was a poor and meagre choice that faced me when I stepped out into an evening.

At first I thought that it would pass. That normal life would return. You people had always been so inventive, so practised at overcoming challenges that I was sure you would overcome this too but as the months went by I started to wonder if that was true.

Quarantines, isolation and lockdowns didn't suit me at all. I hide best in a multitude. When I decide to feed I like to take the weak and the stragglers from the herd. I like crowds

And so, as the streets stayed empty and the bars and nightclubs closed down, I decided that I must leave Europe for a time and travel elsewhere, but where to go? Somewhere crowded and somewhere I might escape notice. Then a thought came to me, if I couldn't become invisible, perhaps I could become ignored, unseen even. Perhaps there was a place where all Europeans were white ghosts, where everyone who looked like me was a foreign devil, a place where we all looked alike?

동쪽

When the seatbelt light is extinguished, everyone else stands. They rise up to their feet determined to continue with the race they call life. I stay where I am. Seated. Sprawled. I know which of us wins the race. I can be the tortoise, let them play at being hares.

Most of the passengers are wearing masks and yet that feels somehow different out here. I'm used to seeing images of masked Asian crowds, so much so that it feels like a part of their national dress.

I'm wearing one too, but for reasons of my own.

We've been in the air for almost fourteen hours. Everyone on the plane looks dreadful; everyone looks like a pale and bloodless ghoul.

We have landed at dusk. The sun falls behind the horizon and a blood-red light streams through the windows and drenches the cabin. The light looks thick and viscous. It feels as if it would run between my fingers and drip to the floor. I wonder what it would taste like?

Flying always makes me feel dirty. Something about the air that is recirculated again and again until it has a vile, mechanical flavour to it. I'm not concerned in the slightest about the virus but I detest feeling un-clean.

Amongst the kaleidoscope of signs in the immigration hall I see one for the washrooms. The sign is in Hangul and

English. An old woman sits on a plastic chair outside the gents. She has a mop and a bucket and there are coins on a plate beside her, a gratuity for keeping the toilets clean but I have no local currency. I drop a 200-euro note on top of her pile. I have no idea what that is worth here. I doubt she does either. She doesn't look at me.

Inside, I wash my hands and face at one of the sinks. In the polished steel mirror my reflection is clear enough. I may not particularly like what I see, but I see it. Bald and rather gaunt, it's the face of an older person, an aesthete, perhaps, or an athlete but Caucasian. Definitely Caucasian. That's the trick of this.

.

I join the queue for foreign passports. It moves, but very slowly. I don't mind. I'm not an impatient man. In fact, I have a bottomless fund of patience.

At last I push my passport across the counter. The immigration official glances down at me. Behind a plastic shield, his face is inscrutable. Bright white neon glares down on us both. I am meant to feel exposed, that nothing can be hidden here, but when they look at me they don't know what they should be looking for, they don't even know what they are looking at.

This authoritarian little man concentrates on his monitor. He studies the words and numbers on his screen. He compares them to my documents, to my passport and my visa. In his own good time he looks back at me and points to my mask. I unhook it from one ear and pull it to the side. He sees a European face, a gaijin, just as he expected. He nods, a fractional dip of his chin and I put my mask back on. He slides a landing slip in between the pages of my passport and waves me through.

.

I have no luggage. No carry-on and nothing in the hold. I sent my baggage and a few possessions on ahead. A house has been rented. A driver has been hired and should be waiting on the other side of the customs hall doors. The doors slide open and I walk through.

Mr Yun is a middle-aged man with a slight stoop. He has a card in his hands with my name on it. His hand is resting on a luggage trolley that we won't be requiring. He wears a mask and a Bluetooth earpiece, a polyester suit and plastic shoes. He looks slightly startled when I walk up to him and he makes a deep and apologetic bow. He tells me he is sorry but he didn't see me, he didn't recognise me in the crowd. He pronounces each word carefully. He strikes me as a pleasant and gentle man. I tell him that I saw him but he replies that I recognised myself, that I saw my name on his card. He has a point.

Mr Yun smells of garlic and ginger and sour, pickled cabbage. He smells so different to milk-fed meat. I hope I'm not going to find the local food difficult.

몇 주

I understand your fear of the virus. I myself was infected but not by Covid-19, indeed, not by a respiratory virus at all but by a blood-borne infection and that, a very long time ago but its affects have been life-changing.

I drank the blood of my maker. I infected myself of my

own volition. We exchanged blood even as we exchanged lives. The contagion affected different people in different ways. The majority who were infected, I later discovered, died. For others the virus made them weak and susceptible to the influence of others. On rare occasion the virus altered its new host in quite remarkable ways and that is what happened in my case.

I became a vampyre.

The cellular clock that tells my body to grow old and eventually die has been stopped. The number of fast-twitch muscle fibres I have compared to slow-twitch fibres has changed; I am quicker and stronger. I need to fuel these changes with a rich source of energy. I need a transfusion of plasma and red and white cells. I need to drink blood. But surely it's not right that I am defined by my food, is it? Is that how you see me and my brothers and sisters, like un-dead vegans continually obsessed with our dietary fads?

There are other side affects. I developed a greater sensitivity to sunlight. I don't turn into dust if I step out into the daylight but I do become sunburned easily. I am short of melatonin.

I don't sleep in a coffin. I have tried it but only as a fetish. It was claustrophobic and uncomfortable and thoroughly unpleasant.

I'm not scared of the cross, although I find most organised religions rather objectionable.

I cast a shadow and I have a reflection; why wouldn't I? I can be killed but forgive me if I don't share the details of exactly how.

So, my virus has produced dramatic biochemical and structural changes but these effects are rare, very rare. The R-number for my particular contagion is .000001. There aren't many vampyres in the world and there never will be.

Under normal conditions, I don't need to feed very often, so at first I am content to stay in my house.

When I was looking through the properties that the letting agent could offer me, this one leapt off the screen. At first I was at a loss as to why but then the penny dropped. With a row of dormer windows, a tile and railing topped tower, three convoluted floors and all safely locked away behind an impressive set of iron gates, the house was what a seventies architect might have built if told to recreate the Addams Family house from memory. It was modern gothic; it had a basement and a cellar. It was almost embarrassingly kitsch. It was perfect.

There is a balcony where I like to sit, shaded from the sun, and from there I can look out over the city, a metropolis built on a river plain and bordered by eight mountains. My house is perched on the upper slopes of one of those mountains. The neighbourhood is prestigious. There are embassies here and the houses of local film stars, or so I am told. The view is impressive. In the daytime I can see a patchwork of tiled roofs and tall brick chimneys, houses built to pay homage to a traditional style by a people who revere their ancestors. Further into the distance, the city disappears into a fug of pollution. As dusk falls the other aspect of my newly adopted city emerges. Neon and laser light, LEDs and video-screens the size of city blocks start to illuminate the downtown district. The colours are bright and garish. It throbs and pulses with light. It's a firework display that has fallen from the night sky and lies broken on the ground.

This place was once known as the Hermit Kingdom. I think its safe to say that it has moved on from that stage.

For the past few days Mr Yun has sat waiting in the car parked outside the gates in case I should have need of him. A mobile phone with his number in the memory sits plugged in to a socket in the kitchen. The kitchen lies undisturbed beneath the faintest layer of dust. The phone is fully charged but unused.

But now, I am irritable. I have a headache. I need to feed.

I am also a little nervous. This is a new country, I find myself in a different society with its own behaviours and mores. It feels odd that I am having to pluck up the courage to explore something new and yet as well as being a vampyre I am also an old man, a very old man. I may be a little set in my ways. It is a long time since I had a fresh experience or a challenge that I hadn't met before. I decide to tread carefully, at least at first.

I ring Mr Yun and tell him I would like to go for a drive.

.

Face hidden behind his mask, Mr Yun holds the car door open for me. He wants to know where we are going and I tell him to show me a little bit of everything, the tourist's tour.

We set off down the mountain. The big car moves slowly down narrow and twisting roads. After a while they open out into wider streets with a gentler slope. These roads are lined with shop fronts with three or four floors of flats and apartments above them. It is a modern, messy, medieval village. The streets aren't yet crowded but there are plenty of people moving around, buying and selling, delivering and taking away. Everyone is wearing a mask.

We drive on. It's as if we travel through time, the buildings become more modern and the streets are wider and busier, there are clipped fir trees along the pavements and Hello Kitty stickers in phone-shop windows. Up ahead I can see the outlines of skyscrapers and tower blocks emerging out of the miasma. The future is there, but it's hazy and indistinct.

Mr Yun asks me where I want to go but I don't know. How would I? We drive down wider and wider streets towards the river until suddenly I feel out of my depth. This is where I need to fish, but this river of people runs too deep and the current is too strong for me yet.

Turn around, I tell Mr Yun. Turn around and let's go home.

.

The world slides past the smoked glass windows of the car. I am socially distanced from the world outside. I have no point of contact, no common reference. Even if I were standing on the street, some barrier would be stopping me from making a connection. It was as if a sheet of rice paper was distorting and dimming what I can see.

We are closer to home now. I don't recognise the streets, but I recognise the feel of the neighbourhood and I am still hungry. Then, amongst all the signs in Asian characters I see a sign in English. It is like hearing your name over the chatter in a crowded room. It jumps out at me.

I tell Mr Yun to pull over.

The shop is quite small but it is perfect for me. The windows are obscured with stickers and notices. There are chillers and fridge cabinets blocking the pavement, milk crates and cardboard boxes are piled up next to the door. Inside the shop is dark and crammed from floor to ceiling with French wine and Danish beer, American crackers and Belgian chocolates. A middle-aged man stands behind the till. He looks at me. He sees just another gaijin, but he smiles and nods. I browse for a minute but I am looking at the shop more than what it has to sell. There is a back door, which is shut. Behind the counter there is only one till and only room for one person. From inside you can hardly see through the windows at all.

I choose a bottle of wine and a piece of cheese. The shopkeeper rings up the total and passes me the card machine. I have no idea how much I have just paid. As I walk out I glance at the notice on the door with opening and closing times.

.

Mr Yun drops me at the house and I tell him that I won't need him again today. I throw the wine and cheese in the bin. I sit on my balcony and watch the light as it changes. I sit there till dusk.

I was careful to remember the route we took from the shop back to my house and so it's quite easy to find my way back to the shop. When I get there the lights are on; the crates and boxes have been taken in. I step inside. The shopkeeper looks at me with no sign of recognition whatsoever. I look around. There is no one else in the shop.

I pick up a packet of meat and gesture to him. He comes toward me. I can feel my body tense.

I need to do this. I need to do it now.

I step past the counter. I am standing next to him. He looks puzzled but the behaviour of gaijin is always hard to understand. I reach around behind his head. I clamp his mask tight to his nose and mouth. His eyes open wide in surprise but the mask stifles him and muffles his shout.

I roll his head back to expose his neck. I stab him twice in the neck. The metal chopstick I brought from the house makes two neat puncture wounds in his carotid artery. I suck at the rich blood pumping from the wound. It is thick, salty and warm. I hear him struggle to breathe behind the mask. He falls unconscious. His heart flutters and I take one last taste before letting him fall to the ground.

I wipe at my lips and chin and my hand comes away red. I pull a mask from my pocket and slip it over my bloodied maw.

I walk home. No one gives me a second glance.

째

Your virus and my virus make killers of us both. With both infections, death is a symptom. From what I can see, when you kill you protest your innocence but The Nineteen has been with you for long enough now for everyone to know how it spreads, just how and when you infect each other. At least I accept my guilt.

Wash your hands as much as you like. If I want your life, I will take it.

.

I spend the next few days exploring further afield. I'm sure Mr Yun thinks that I am sightseeing and in a way I am. I'm also stalking for my next kill. It's exciting. Back in Europe I had become a creature of habit, set in my ways. Here I can reinvent myself. I don't have to follow old behaviours and customs. I can do just as I will.

And this place offers such richness and variety. It is ancient and modern. It is a feudal society interconnected by 5G. It's a medieval way of life lit by LEDs. Scooters and mopeds have replaced donkeys. Temples of the old religion sit side by side with palaces of consumerism. Monks and malls look disdainfully at each other. You could get lost here. And I do.

Remember I said I liked crowds? This place has one of the highest population densities on earth.

Most people wear masks and many of them wear gloves and even coveralls but they can't social-distance from each other. The entire city is one big crowd. People exist cheek by jowl. It is partly because of this that I can stay unnoticed. To cope with living on top of each other, people simply filter most other people out. They distinguish their own immediate family from the herd but almost no one else.

I watch the throng in a crowded street. They ignore

each other. Their concept of personal space is almost nil. It isn't as if they barge or bump each other in a rude way, they just ignore each other and that is with members of their own race, their own community. I am ignored with such determination that I almost become invisible. A white ghost; a gweilo.

로

On the return from one of our drives through the metropolis we pass a group of men erecting a tent by the side of the street and unloading tables and chairs from a lorry. Mr Yun tells me it is one of the old traditions that has survived into the modern age and became popular again. He tells me what will happen here tonight. It's a piece of cultural history wrapped in a plastic tarp and sitting under a space heater. I find the idea rather appealing. I think it will fit my purpose rather well.

In Europe I loved café culture and in particular the early evening ritual they call la passeggiata, that leisurely stroll from bar to bar. It's a time for people to parade and flaunt themselves and to be noticed. Often to be noticed by me. We eat with our eyes after all. It sounds to me as if they are putting up this tent for a very similar purpose. I should definitely taste the local nightlife.

·

When I was planning this adventure I thought that having a driver would be a huge advantage, at least until I had settled in and got my bearings but I should have thought harder and longer; I should have done a little more research.

I had not expected Mr Yun to be sitting in the car outside my gates from dawn till dusk but that is exactly what he does. That is what drivers do here. They are just seen as part of the car, like a wheel or the boot lid.

I have had staff and servants before and yes, it all starts out splendidly but as time goes by I start to realise that this person, this butler or major domo, maid or housekeeper or yes, driver, is watching all the time. I don't mind if they see me develop an interest in orchids or Japanese brush calligraphy, in early renaissance chamber music or pop art but I do mind if there is a chance of them watching me eat. I mind if there is a likelihood that they may deduce who, or what, if you wish to be nasty, they are working for.

This has played out in a number of different ways over the years. Unfortunately for many of them, terminating their contract of employment has proved to be a rather harsher process then they might have hoped for or expected. Having said that, I can remember two who have drunk my blood and gone on to live their own lives in this altered state but I don't see Mr Yun as a natural candidate for this unusual life. I wonder what I should do?

.

I am irritable. I have a headache. I need to feed.

Once again you find me on my balcony looking out over the city. I am of such an age that it becomes difficult for me to remain interested in the world and yet here I am, living in interesting times. That's no curse for me; it's a blessing. The march of time is often just the progress of a mind from a state of excitement and fascination to one of boredom and disinterest but here, as I float over their world, I see enough to capture my attention. The virus still slaughters them in their droves. I have lived through plagues and pandemics before but this one is different. Their technology allows them to be aware of every death, every sickness and every moment of mourning. These people who have distanced themselves from strangers, from all those other than their family, walk around with a smartphone in their pocket that continually updates them on how many have died today; how many of this age group, how many from this neighbourhood, how many men and how many women. They are forced to acknowledge each and every stranger's demise. They are caught in the net, held captive by the web. Humans can deal with human experience but this goes beyond that. It is as if they have become cyborgs implanted with a chip that streams anxiety and distress directly into their cortex; no filters, no looking away and no release. A little less than purely human, they are profiles and avatars and all the more vulnerable for it. They are hacked by emotion and infected with unease.

I breathe in the dirty, dusty air. I am irritable. I have a headache.

Floating above this infected city I feel closer to the human condition. My virus is of the blood. It is visceral. When you die of my contagion you will be able to look me in the eye, you will feel my arms around you and my mouth on your flesh. It is an intimate thing and it will just be the two of us, just you and me embracing.

.

I need to feed.

I plan to make a little theatre to go with tonight's meal,

a dinner dance, supper and a play if you will. I tell Mr Yun I am not felling well and I send him home. He asks me if I think I have caught the virus and I assure him that I do not. He mumbles behind his mask. He will see me again tomorrow at the usual time.

I watch the car as it begins its smooth descent of the hill. He seems such a nice man.

I dress carefully and smartly in Prada and Armani. I put a few things into a Louis Vuitton bag. I realise it is still early. I must be excited. What an unfamiliar emotion.

.

When the sky has turned a rich, regal purple and the brighter lights of the centre are easily seen I use the mobile to call a taxi.

The driver drops me just around the corner from the pojangmacha; the drinking tent. I pay by card. The man on the door lets me in without any hesitation although it seems unlikely they have many western customers. Inside it stinks of cigarette smoke and sweat and beer and soju. Condensation drips from the ceiling. The floor is made of interlocking vinyl tiles that are soaked in spilled alcohol and covered in discarded facemasks. People are packed together like sushi in a bento box. At the moment they are still divided into single-sex tables but that all seems about to end. There are no rules in here. Rules are left at the door. No one is obeying the instructions regarding The Nineteen, no one is kow-towing to their superior and no one is drinking responsibly. This is a medieval release from modern constraints. This is a race to insensibility. It is so noisy that I doubt the barman could have understood me even if we spoke the same language. I point to the bottles of soju and hold up two fingers. He hands me two bottles. I pass him my card. He points to an empty table in the corner. The plastic stool is uncomfortable. The vinyl tablecloth has been wiped clean but the tin ashtray is still full of wet paper tissues and nicotine yellow cigarette butts. I put the two bottles of soju on the table and two glasses. I look at my watch. I make quite a big deal of looking at my watch.

The women's tables are as loud as the men's. Everyone laughs too loud. They cover their mouths with their hands when they giggle but not because of the virus. Waitresses deliver bowls of chicken feet and noodles to the tables, but not to mine. Men and women start to look openly at each other, appraising and offering. The boundaries are becoming blurred. A young man sets off towards a table of women but then swerves to one side and scuttles towards the restrooms. His friends shriek with laughter.

I look at my watch again. I can't see if anyone is watching me, but I know that someone will be. There always is.

The place is full now. All the tables are packed. The 'necktie army' of office workers stands three deep at the bar. The girls have abandoned coy glances in favour of blatantly pointing and giggling. The lid is about to come off the social pressure cooker. I imagine the air must be thick with The Nineteen and it doesn't look as if a single soul cares.

I can feel my pulse pounding as if I were drunk. The atmosphere is intoxicating. I loved la passeggiata but this is somehow much more raw, less civilised, dirtier. Men and women are moving between tables now. I see one couple steal a furtive kiss. I check my watch. This last time should do it. I have a sense for these things.

I had hoped that a woman would approach me but it doesn't really matter. He is young and good-looking and his eyes are already glazed with glasses of beer or soju.

In broken English he asks me if I am waiting for someone. I shrug and try to look a little sad. I can smell his aftershave and beneath that, him.

He asks if he can join me and I nod. I push one of the bottles across the table as he sits. We pour and drink together. At least, he does. I spill mine on the floor at my feet.

He tells me he is a model. Of course he is. He asks me if I was expecting to meet someone who didn't show up and I nod a little sadly.

I concentrate on him now. I watch him very closely. Being studied makes him flush with pleasure.

He drinks again. This will need to happen soon. Once he is very drunk things will get more difficult. Both soju bottles are empty now. Just one more, he asks. One more before what, I wonder. Surely he hasn't guessed.

He comes back from the bar with two bottles. He is a little unsteady on his feet. He reaches out across the table and takes my hand. He frowns. He tells me that I am very cold but I smile and shrug off his concern. It must be now. I smile into his eyes and ask him if we should take the drink outside. At first he looks confused so I ask him again. He flushes at my western forwardness, my lack of morals but he nods his head. He takes the soju. I bring my bag.

After the brightness inside the tent it seems very dark outside. We have stepped out into an alley and there are only a few lighted signs and a reflected glow from a street light on the corner.

He goes to kiss me but I push him further back into the dark. He is shorter than me but broad across his shoulders.

I put my hand on his jaw and stroke his neck. His breath is sour with drink.

I take one of the bottles from his hand and hold it up as if to toast him. He says something in a language I don't understand. Smiling, I drop the bottle.

It falls and smashes on the pavement.

I duck down and grab the broken neck. I am very fast.

As I rise I jab the broken glass into his throat and twist. His eyes open wide. Blood gushes from the wound.

I put my mouth to the gash and drink.

For a moment he struggles then he leans in to me and we sway like dancers.

His blood soaks me.

I pull his empty body further into the alley and push it behind a bin.

I open the Vuitton bag and pull out what is inside it. Less then two minutes later I walk out of the alley and past the tent.

The man on the door looks at me but all he sees is a figure shrouded in a full HAZMAT suit, mask, gloves and overshoes. My stained clothes and bloody face are hidden. I walk through the crowd outside the tent.

A little further on I check Google maps on my phone. I'm only a couple of miles from home. I decide to walk and enjoy the evening air.

인

One of the reasons I chose this particular city was the vast amount of it that is actually underground, not just a transport system but shops, bars and restaurants, a library and, I believe, at lest three swimming pools. It is an underground metropolis where the sun never shines. Like Morlocks the locals disappear down stairways and elevators to live a subterranean life, and I can follow them there.

·

Mr Yun drops me at one of the big, international hotels. I walk out of a side entrance and disappear down a stairway into the under-city.

The stairway brings me out in one of the side streets of the city beneath. There are ordinary little shops lining the tunnel. A shop window and some display racks outside; inside sits an elderly woman waiting for either a customer or closing time. The shops sell toiletries, bags, phone accessories and cameras, phone contracts, polyester jumpers, plastic shoes and nylon slippers, German shampoos and French hair dye, sportswear, socks and tights. The floor of the corridor is paved in slabs of pink polished granite. The ceiling is panelled with neon tubes and dotted with cameras and emergency lighting. Shoppers amble in pairs, usually young women looking more as if they are here to pass time than spend money.

There are overhead signs promising bigger malls, better shopping experiences, and so I follow them.

The spaces get bigger. The crowds get bigger to fill up the spaces. Everyone is wearing a mask, myself included. There are 'pavement' cafes with people drinking coffee. There are signs to movie theatres and a public library. My original enthusiasm is starting to wane. For all of its subterranean nature, it is very lit and very open. Far too exposed for my taste. After exploring for a couple of hours I think I may as well turn around and retrace my steps.

.

I'm approaching the smaller tunnel that leads back to where I entered this rabbit hole when I notice that the walkers and shoppers are bunching up. The crowd should be thinning out but it appears to be getting thicker.

There is a man in a HAZMAT suit with a sash over his shoulder and a temperature reader in his hand. In his other hand he holds a tablet and he concentrates on the screen. There doesn't feel to be any danger here but none the less I tense a little.

I'm about twenty-five meters from him now. He isn't stopping anyone. I have no reason for concern.

I walk slowly and purposefully. I look around, just as any shopper would. There is nothing to alarm me here.

He looks up from his screen. He looks me straight in the eye. He beckons me towards him.

I take the last few steps.

I stand in front of him.

He is in his thirties with an ordinary, open face but there is tension around his eyes and his lips are hard pressed together. He is trembling a little. I can smell the fear on him.

He raises the digital thermometer and points it at my forehead. We stand in a little bubble of silence and immobility. The world passes by on either side like the river flowing past a rock.

He shows me the digital readout. 22deg C.

Quietly he tells me that he knows what I am. Not who,

but what. He says that I am to expect him at my house this evening, at midnight.

Fascinated by his audacity I lean towards him and breath deeply in. I take in his scent. His courage wavers. He steps back and as he waves me past, I look down at the screen of his tablet. It is showing this mall, the very part of it that we are in. It must be the feed from one of the CCTV cameras in the ceiling.

I give him the smallest bow as I walk away back towards the hotel and Mr Yun.

끝

I sit on my balcony and look out over the city. The sun drops through the sky like a blood-red cherry. I wonder what is happening. I wonder what has happened. Will a crowd march up the road with pitchforks and firebrands or will that one little man knock politely on my door?

Time passes slowly. The neighbouring roofs fade into blackness, the bright lights of downtown glitter in the night. By eleven it is pitch black around me and I can see the stars in the sky.

An hour later the gate buzzer goes. I haven't heard a car and I didn't hear him walk up the hill. He must be wearing rubber-soled shoes.

I go downstairs to the hallway and look at him on the entry phone. It's him. An unassuming little man with his courage screwed down tight.

I buzz the gate open and then watch on the other camera as he climbs the steps to the porch. No pitchfork, no firebrand.

I open the door for him and then stand back. He pauses

on the threshold. He holds a mask in one hand and asks me if he should put it on but I shake my head and beckon him in. He is reluctant, as if he fears standing in an enclosed space without his mask on more than he fears sharing that space with a vampire, for he surely knows exactly what I am.

He follows me through into the main hall of the house, a large space empty of furniture but where I have put a few of the things I shipped over from Europe. There is a Rembrandt study for The Night Watch leaning against the wall and a scroll of Soseki's brush calligraphy pinned to the back of a door. On the mantle above the fireplace is a katana sword on a lacquered stand. In the open grate are the ashes of the ruined suit that I wore to the pojangmacha. There is a maquette of a Degas ballerina in the corner.

There are no chairs. We stand in front of each other. He keeps his distance. At last he speaks.

He tells me that he works as a contact tracer. He was at the airport when I arrived. He scanned my temperature while my passport was being checked. I don't have a temperature, I reply. No, he says, you don't, do you.

I walk to the windows and look out into the night.

Behind me, I hear him speak. He tells me that he guessed what I might be then but he needed to be sure. As a contact tracer he has access to all the data that is collected on the population. He can search for anything. He can see anything. He started to search for me.

I ask him why. He doesn't reply but I already know. I have been here before. It's rather sad really.

For a time, for a few days, there was no sign of me, he says, but then one of my credit cards was used in a shop where the following day the police reported a murder.

Then I disappeared again.

He is warming to the story now. He thinks he's been clever and he wants me to know it. He wants me to know I am trapped. He really should have bought a pitchfork.

I watch his reflection in the glass.

The card was used again, he says, to pay for a taxi and in a soju bar and then a mobile phone registered to my account logged on to the 5G network and travelled at walking pace from the bar to this house. The next morning a young man's body was found in an alley behind the bar. He had been brutally killed but of course, says my guest, you know that.

I ask him once again what he wants but it seems the whole of the story has to play out before he will confess to that.

Apparently he contacted a friend in the police and enquired about the two killings. His friend told him that there were no suspects and that the killer appeared to have vanished unseen, like a ghost.

He stands beside me now. We look at the motionless garden together.

He asks me to understand what it is that he has done and why. He tells me that over the last year he has seen thousands of people die, probably he has seen more death than me. He can't stand the idea of catching The Nineteen. It terrifies him. It scares him more than me. I doubt that he should feel that way but now is not the time to share that thought with him. There is one thing I need to know before then.

Where will the story go now, I wonder? It seems strange that I was playing my part in front of such an attentive audience and was thoroughly unaware of it. If I had known

I would have been a little more dramatic to reward this viewer up in the gallery.

My visitor tells me that he pulled my car's registration number from the database and added it to the vehicles that the ANPR system was looking for. He got my photo from immigration and uploaded that to the city's facial recognition database and the CCTV cameras. The systems that he normally used to contact-trace the virus were now all looking for me as well.

I walk over to stand by the fireplace. I lean on it. I think it makes me look rather patrician. What do you want, I ask him. He wants me to bite him, he replies. To drink his blood so that he may become immortal and live without fear of death.

It's always so disappointing. For them to think that I would share my virus indiscriminately, with just anyone. Do they think that I would be the sort of person who would stand in a crowd without a mask? Would I cough on a stranger? Would I stand in a crowded room shedding my spores?

In any event, he has fallen victim to fake news, I don't need to drink his blood; he needs to drink mine. It seems even this man whose job it is to contain a virus doesn't really understand how they spread.

I ask him who else knows.

No one, he replies, and seals his fate.

I walk slowly towards him. I smile sadly. It is nice to be appreciated, to be the focus of all this attention. It is a shame that it's all for the wrong reasons.

He looks over my shoulder and sees that the katana is no longer on its stand.

He tilts his head to one side exposing his neck. He bows

his head.

Please, he says quietly.

I wonder what he means.

끝

I think I will return to Europe. The computers see me too clearly here; the cameras, the data, all that surveillance. It's like an eye that never blinks. I can walk through the people and they look the other way, they choose not to see me. My face gets lost in the crowd. The machine doesn't lose my face. It watches me as dispassionately as I watch the people that built it.

Watching without caring. It is as cruel as I am.

Anyway, it has been an interesting adventure but I think it has run its course.

They say that The Nineteen still rages in the old country but I'm sure they are exaggerating.

I will need Mr Yun to drive me to the airport. I will leave him the Rembrandt and his life as gifts.

In time people will learn what I did here. They might come to realise what I am and perhaps they will come to my house, to this gothic folly, to burn it down in the old, traditional way; exorcising the white ghost.

I wonder if they will bring pitchforks?

# WISH LIST

ELLIE BOLITHO was a happy soul.

There would be some who didn't reckon her life much to write home about but Ellie was content. She lived in a cottage in Perrancoombe Woods at the end of a long, rutted and muddy track. Ellie had a bird's nest of grey hair, a pretty little nose and a body that she might call plump but was definitely becoming fat. However, what people mostly remembered about Ellie was her laugh. Ellie's laugh was like a canary let free from its cage. Ellie's laugh fluttered and flapped around a room and brightened the day of everyone who heard it.

Ellie lived on her small pension with half a dozen geese and a constantly changing number of cats. Not so many that they would imply a degree of senility but certainly enough to show that she was a woman who was very fond of cats.

Ellie also had a sister.

Ellie's sister disliked geese, wasn't particularly fond of cats and lived comfortably on her salary. The two women had been born nine years apart and for the first part of their lives Ellie had looked after her little sister but then, somewhere along the road, the roles had been reversed and her younger sister had decided that she should be the one that was in charge.

Ellie's sister paid regular visits, which both woman referred to as 'coming for tea', but both knew were for the younger woman to keep an eye on her older sibling.

'Is that a new dent?' said her sister looking at the rear bumper of Ellie's little car.

Ellie explained that the concrete bollards in the supermarket car park were too low and not easy to see. Her sister looked at a long scrape down the side of the car. There was red paint in the scratch.

'Did you hit another car?' she asked.

'I don't think so. Perhaps someone parked too close to me? I don't remember bumping into anyone.'

Ellie's sister looked exasperated. 'You can't keep having accidents. Someone will report you, or worse.'

Ellie pushed her hands deep into the pocket of her apron. 'I'll be careful,' she murmured. 'I will.'

'You think it's just a little scrape but some people like to look after their cars,' and both women looked at the gleaming black BMW that was parked in Ellie's drive.

'You wouldn't be happy to get a scratch on yours, would you?' Ellie said and let a little laugh flutter into the air but her sister didn't look amused.

.

A fortnight later the BMW made its way gingerly down the lane again, carefully avoiding the potholes and the puddles.

Ellie saw her through the kitchen window and set off

to meet her, still drying her hands on a tea towel. Her idea had been to distract her somehow but the plan failed.

'What have you done?' asked her sister as she shooed away the hissing geese. Ellie's little silver car was not parked outside her cottage but, rather suspiciously, it was parked in the barn and the barn doors were closed. Ellie wanted to reply that she had done nothing but it sounded rather too much like the answer a guilty child might give.

'The man was very nice about it,' she said. 'His lorry wasn't damaged at all. They are very strong, those big lorries.'

Ellie's sister sighed and swung the barn door open. The little silver car had lost one of its driving mirrors and the passenger door now curved inwards where once it had bulged out.

'I think we need to have a talk,' said her sister. 'A serious talk,' and she led Ellie back towards the cottage. 'Let's get the kettle on.'

While they waited for the kettle to start singing on the hob the two women sat at the table in Ellie's kitchen. Ellie began to wring her hands, still wrapped in the tea towel. These little talks seldom went well. Two of the cats watched from the depths of an over-stuffed wing chair with what might have been sympathy.

'I know you don't want to hear this but I think it might be time you put the car away.'

'It's in the barn. You've just seen it,' replied Ellie rather too quickly and her bright laugh circled the room for a second.

'You know what I mean,' said her sister through a thin smile.

'I do,' said Ellie. 'But I need to get to the shops. I'm not going on the bus with bags of shopping.'

'But if you had an accident, a proper accident?'

'I'll be careful.'

'No. I mean what if you hurt someone else? What if someone got hurt? Even if you have a small bump your insurance will go up. Could you afford that?'

Outside an autumn breeze ambled through the trees behind the cottage and kicked up the leaves on the little patch of lawn. The geese watched as it wandered off into the woods.

'I like living here,' said Ellie. 'It's my home.'

'I know,' said her sister. 'I know. But we need to be realistic. '

The women sat for a moment, avoiding catching each other's eye. They sat on opposite shores of a flat, grey lake of silence.

'I'll think about it,' said Ellie in a small voice.

'So will I,' said her sister.

Barely a week passed before they were sitting together in the kitchen again.

'I've decided. I want you to give me the car keys,' said her sister. 'I've been thinking about this and, what are we going to do? Wait until you have a serious accident? Wait until you are in hospital or the police are at the door?'

Ellie opened her mouth but her sister shushed her.

'I know what your car means to you. I know it means your independence...' Ellie began to speak but her sister carried on. 'I know it means your independence but I think there's a way to keep living here but not use your car.

Wouldn't that be for the best? Lord knows, I don't want you coming to live with me, do I?' and she laughed but her eyes were flinty and serious. 'Let's try it for a month and see how you manage. We won't sell the car, just SORN it. Then if things…'

Ellie looked suspiciously at her sibling. 'What's a SORN?'

'It just means you don't have to tax or insure your car while you're not using it.'

'And it's another way of making sure I can't drive. You know, in case I had another set of keys in a drawer somewhere,' said Ellie proving that she was a lot more shrewd than she sometimes looked.

'I just want what's best for you.'

'Do you? Well I really don't know that it feels that way but I'm sure you are just doing your best.'

The younger sister bridled. 'What do you actually use the car for?' she asked.

'I go visiting friends.'

'Not since Noreen died and Shirley went into that home, and that was months and months ago.'

'I go for my check up at the doctors. I drive there.'

'I can take you,' said her sister and then, 'or you can get a cab,' after she had thought about it a bit longer.

'It's nice to get out.'

'You'd rather be here with your cats.'

The women sipped at their tea. Ellie offered her sister a biscuit.

'The shops,' said Ellie just as her sister said, 'Just shopping, isn't it.'

Ellie's sister looked rather pleased with herself. 'So, it isn't a problem then,' she said.

'What do you mean?'

'No one goes to the shops anymore. Everyone shops online.'

'Not me,' said Ellie.

'You will.'

Ellie's sister turned her chair away from the table and she started to rummage around in the plants and pottery and old postcards that filled the kitchen windowsill. At last she found a length of telephone wire and traced it back to a phone socket that was screwed against the window frame. 'You see,' she said. 'I remembered this.'

The socket had two jacks, one had the phone lead plugged into it and the other was an Ethernet port. Thanks to a European digital infrastructure development fund that needed spending and an enthusiastic Openreach engineer, Ellie's cottage had broadband. She wasn't on mains drainage and she wasn't on the gas but she had an Internet download speed of just over 25Mbps.

'I don't have a computer,' said Ellie. 'You do need a computer, don't you?'

Ellie's sister agreed that you did need a computer. 'Let me buy one for you. It's the least I can do in the circumstances,' and although Ellie liked to think that she was independent and could pay for her own things she graciously accepted her sister's offer. 'In the circumstances,' she said with a smile.

They agreed to go shopping together next week. 'We can look at the Apple shop in town or there is a PC World, out by the roundabout.'

'Do I need a fancy one?' asked Ellie.

'Computer?'

'Yes.'

'You get what you pay for, don't you,' replied her sister.

.

'Whose car shall we go in?' asked Ellie when her sister came to pick her up. 'I can drive if you want.' Her laugh fluttered amongst the dead leaves floating in the air until it caught sight of Ellie's sister's scowl and fell to the ground like a wet rag.

'Put your seat belt on,' said Ellie's sister as she settled into the driving seat.

They went to PC World first because it was on the way.

When they started looking at the display of laptops they realised that neither of them knew very much about computers at all. This came as no surprise to Ellie but her sister had assumed that she would understand what made one different from the next and which might be the best to choose.

'So which of these two is the best one?' asked Ellie's sister.

'It depends what you want to do with it,' said the assistant.

'What's a RAM?' asked Ellie.

The assistant gave her a quizzical look. 'Memory,' he said.

'Is that important? To have a lot of memory, is that good?'

'What are you going to use it for?' asked the assistant.

'Shopping.'

The assistant slowly nodded his head. 'They're all good for that. Maybe this one? It's on offer.'

'What about that one?'

'Oh yeah,' he said, yawning. 'That's good too.'

The women left the store empty-handed and Ellie's sister drove quite quickly out of the store's car park. The BMW actually bounced a little as it went over the speed bump and a man pushing a shopping trolley glared at them and wagged his finger in admonishment.

'Careful,' said Ellie. 'You don't want to hit anything, do you?' but then she pursed her lips with her laugh safely behind them. 'Where are we going now?' she asked, as they pulled out of the car park.

''We'll go and look at the Apple store. They are a bit pricy, but they are good.'

It only took them ten minutes to drive into town and around to the multi-story. There was very little traffic on the roads and the car park, when they got there, was more than half empty.

The Apple shop was on the other side of town, near the cathedral. Ellie and her sister walked down the ramp and out on to the High Street.

'There's a lot of empty shops, aren't there?' said Ellie's sister. 'Even most of the shoe shops have gone and I thought they would outlast everyone.'

'It looks like nothing but coffee shops and charity shops now. That's pretty much all that's left.'

'Some of the little ones are still doing all right. Let's cut through the Warrens. There used to be some nice shops in there.'

The Warrens was a maze of narrow, twisted alleyways filled with quirky shops and vegan tearooms. The alleys were too narrow for cars so racks of clothes and café tables, baskets of organic veg and piles of bric-a-brac spilled out on to the pavements. There was an art shop and picture framers, a hippy boutique and a posh frock shop. There were antique shops and junk shops and sometimes it was difficult to tell the difference between the two.

One shop like that was called, "Cave of Wonders".

'Stop. Stop. Stop, stop,' said Ellie and she grabbed her sisters arm. 'That's a laptop in there, isn't it? Isn't that one?' and she pointed to a silver laptop at the back of the window's display case.

Ellie's sister frowned.

'We're not getting one from here,' she said.

'If it works, why not?'

'I'm not buying a second-hand one. I'll get you a new one, but I won't buy an old one. What if it breaks? What then?'

'Let's just a have a look,' said Ellie, and she pushed her way past her sister and in through the door of the shop.

Ellie could see where the shop had got its name. The Cave of Wonders was dark and high-ceilinged. Its nooks had crannies and its alcoves had corners into which objects had been tucked away. Every surface had items piled upon it and all of that stuff was for sale. Some bits looked valuable and some worthless, some looked collectable and some best ignored. It was a treasure trove as long as your definition of "treasure" was wide.

Ellie's sister came into the shop behind her. Still scowling she looked around and reached out to examine a random object, in this case a cut-crystal rummer. Ellie put her hand out to stop her sister and pointed to a big notice above the till.

Lovely to look at,
Delightful to hold,
If you break it,

Consider it sold.

'Afternoon,' said the young man at the till. 'Feel free to browse, but…' and he pointed up at the notice.

'We were wondering about the laptop that's in the window. We couldn't see a price on it,' said Ellie. Her sister rolled her eyes and picked up an enamelled tea caddy that she studied closely. This conversation was nothing to do with her.

The young man came out from behind the counter, picking his way carefully between the piles. He peered into the window. 'I put that out this morning. I found it in the stock room at the back.'

'Is it for sale?'

He shrugged. 'Why else would it be here?'

'This isn't your shop then?'

'I just do a couple of days a week. Would you like to have a look at it?'

Ellie said that she would and the young man snaked his arm through piles of video games and ranks of smart phones until he managed to get to it and handed it to Ellie.

'It works alright does it?'

'I should think so.'

'Well, if you don't know…' said Ellie's sister from the shadows.

'Everything electrical has been checked over and the phones and computers come with a warranty,' he said rather prissily.

'I'd rather not buy a new one if we could avoid it,' said Ellie. 'It's better for the planet, isn't it?' and Ellie's sister rolled her eyes again. 'If I'm paying we are getting a new one,' she said.

The young man put the laptop down on the counter.

Ellie brushed her fingers across its case and then snatched them back. 'Ooh,' she said. 'It tingled.'

Just static I should think,' he said smiling. 'You get that sometimes.' He opened the laptop and pressed the power button. A little gear wheel appeared in the middle of the screen and began to spin. Ellie and the young man watched it for a minute and then, sure enough, the desktop opened. It was a picture of a kitten.

'Look,' said Ellie, laughing. 'It's kismet. 'This is the one we are meant to get or why would it have a kitten on it?'

The young man's eyes twinkled as Ellie's laugh fluttered around the room. 'She could be right, you know,' he said to Ellie's sister who just half-closed her eyes and shook her head in frustration. 'Is it the right spec or whatever they call it?' she asked.

'What do you want it for?'

'Shopping,' said both women at the same time.

'It'll be perfect,' he said.

'I still think we should get a new one.'

'Then I'll buy it,' said Ellie. 'How much is it?'

·

The following day, Ellie's nephew came around and set up the computer, the router and everything else she needed. He even set up a few online shopping accounts for her groceries and anything else she might need.

'Where did you get the laptop from?' he asked.

Ellie asked him if there was anything wrong with it and he said that there wasn't, it all seemed fine, but it was an odd machine and he'd not seen one quite like it before. 'At least it's not running Windows 10,' he said, but Ellie didn't know what he meant by that and she didn't like to ask.

'Is there anything else I can do while I'm here?' he asked. What about internet banking or Netflix or Facebook or something?'

Ellie remembered that popping in to the bank or using a cash machine wasn't going to be so easy if she wasn't driving so she said yes to the online banking. When he explained Facebook to her, she said, 'Why would anyone want that?' As far as Netflix was concerned, she said she would make do with her television.

Her nephew scribbled his number on a scrap of paper and told Ellie that he would be happy to come back if there was anything she needed help with. Ellie thanked him with a big piece of homemade chocolate cake and a hug.

When she was alone with her cats, Ellie looked from the empty hook by the door where her car keys used to hang to the laptop sitting on her kitchen table. She took a deep breath that caught in her chest and made the cat on her lap reach up with a comforting paw and pat at her. Life was going to be different, wasn't it? Although it had been nice to get out and about it had sometimes been a worry too. If she was honest, the little accidents had scared her and she knew that her driving was getting worse. It was, as her sister said, only a matter of time before something serious happened, but she would never have admitted that to anyone.

But... with the car in the garage and the car keys on her sister's pocket Ellie felt more alone than she had for a long, long time. She stroked the cat on her lap until it purred like a tiny engine.

'We just need to get used to it, don't we?' she said to herself. 'It's just something new. It'll be fine.' And the cat purred in agreement.

She opened the laptop and pressed the power button. It whirred and clicked for a moment and then the desktop lit up with the picture of the kitten and the icons that her nephew had left behind, Tesco and Amazon and NatWest and the others. They looked like places on a map, unconnected by roads. She leant her elbows on the table and put her chin in her hands and peered at the screen a while longer. She put her finger on the track pad and steered the big grey cursor from Tesco to Argos and back again, being careful not to drive over the kitten's nose. She discovered that her nephew had set up an email account and a Hotmail address for her but she didn't have any Contacts to write to so she closed that icon almost as soon as she had opened it. She leaned in towards the screen and the cat on her lap found herself squeezed against the table but refused to give up her favourite place just because of a little discomfort.

Ellie took a deep breath and clicked on the Tesco icon.

The site had shopping baskets and drop-down menus; it had a place to put her shopping list and search for the stuff that was on it. It had sections that were a bit like all the different aisles that you'd find in the shop. Ellie thought that she could soon get the hang of this and she still thought that almost two hours later when she signed out of the site, her first shopping order being done.

Ellie sighed and pushed her chair back from the table and the cat uncurled herself and jumped up next to the laptop. She pushed her nose up against the open screen and rubbed her cheek against the side before suddenly hissing and arching her back. She jumped off the table and trotted out of the kitchen door, her tail swishing like a flag in the wind.

'What's wrong?' Ellie called out after her but the cat didn't even look over her shoulder.

.

'Shouldn't it be a Tesco van?' asked Ellie.

'I just deliver what I'm told, Mrs Bolitho. Perhaps they are too busy.'

A plain white van was parked in her drive and her Tesco shopping was sitting just outside the kitchen door in a big, blue plastic crate.

'Is it all there?' asked Ellie peering into the crate.

'If that's what you asked for, Mrs Bolitho. If that's what you wanted, that's what you've got,' and he smiled. A big, fat, dimple-making smile. 'Shall I bring it in for you?'

Conscious of the state of her kitchen, Ellie said no thank you; she would bring it in her self.

'Then I'll wish you a good day, Mrs Bolitho. I will see you again, I'm sure,' and with a twinkle in his eye, he turned and jogged off back towards his van. What a nice man, thought Ellie, and dragged her crate of food into the kitchen.

Two of the cats sniffed at it suspiciously and it was only then that she realised the geese hadn't reacted to the deliveryman. They hadn't honked at his arrival, indeed they hadn't cackled or hissed at him at all. They had watched from the far side of the garden, and they had watched in silence.

Ellie shook her head. Funny things, geese.

For the next few days, life went on as normal. Ellie realised that she didn't use her car all that often. She pottered in the garden and she worked in the vegetable bed. She sat in the weak sunshine and read her book. She walked in the woods behind her cottage and she watched her cats as her cats watched the birds that came down to the feeder she had hung from a tree. Life is little things happening one after another.

On the Friday she decided to bake a cake and she found out that she had run out of flour.

When she turned the laptop on to do another shop, she saw that she had received an email. Clicking on it, Ellie learnt that the person who had sent the email wondered if Ellie would like a felt cat-cocoon. In fact what they said was, "Find Cat Beds To Treat And Care For Your Pets Today. We Have Just The Right Thing For Your Pets." Which didn't surprise Ellie as much as the fact that this person knew Ellie had pets. In fact, they seemed to know she had cats. How did they know that? It was like magic.

She sat down with a cup of tea in one hand and a cat on her lap – although none of them would sit up on the table next to the laptop – and made out her order. Her fingers pecked at the keyboard like a chicken picking grain.

Flour, obviously. Less milk than last time, she'd had to throw a litre away. Sausages, this week, she thought; there is something lovely about a sizzling sausage. Wet cat food, she still had a half a bag of the dry. Ginger biscuits, to go with the tea. Tea! She'd almost forgotten to buy tea.

Just an hour later, with the satisfied sigh that goes with a job well done, Ellie clicked the last click on her Tesco order and stretched back in her chair. The cat on her lap anchored itself with sharp claws that went straight through Ellie's jogging bottoms.

'Oh,' she said to the sprawled feline. 'I suppose you'd

like a cat cave, would you?' and she scratched the soft hairs on its stomach. The cat purred and half-closed its eyes, which clenched the deal.

The email had a link that took Ellie to a whole page of cat beds on Amazon and although, if she had thought about it, she knew her cats weren't short of places to sleep, she bought one anyway – and a matching scratching post.

.

It was the same delivery driver as last time.

By the time Ellie had come down to answer the doorbell, her Tesco crate was on the doorstep and the deliveryman was coming back down the drive from his van balancing one little brown cardboard box on top of a much bigger one. 'Hello, Mrs Bolitho,' he called from behind the parcels. 'Told you I would see you soon, didn't I.' He put the boxes down on the step and this time Ellie took a good look at him.

He had a ponytail and a beard. The beard was teased into a point and the ponytail came from quite high up on his head.

'Shall I bring these inside for you, Mrs Bolitho?'

He was a little overweight. He had more than one spare tyre around his waist; more like three.

Ellie said it was fine; he could leave them there. She really must get the kitchen tidy, she thought.

He smiled a lot. It was a good smile. His eyes twinkled and his teeth shone.

'My name is Dwayne,' he said. 'See, it says it on my badge here,' and he grabbed his plastic name badge on his polyester jumper and held it out towards Ellie; the jumper stretching like elastic.

'Hello, Dwayne,' said Ellie. 'Call me Ellie.'

'I best be on my way, Mrs Bolitho. Big round today.'

Dwayne's skin was as dark and glossy as bonfire toffee.

'Have a nice day then,' said Ellie and she picked up the bigger of the two Amazon parcels and took it into the house.

．

The cats really liked their new scratching post and the cat cave proved to be very popular; so popular that they were constantly squabbling over it so Ellie bought three more.

She thought it would be nice to buy something for the geese too but it turns out there aren't many gifts suitable for geese and Ellie became distracted and ended up buying a Cosy Cuddly Goose Hot Water Bottle Cover. She thought it looked lovely and her old hot water bottle cover was on the way out so it wasn't a silly purchase, it was something that she really needed, at least that is what she told herself.

On the Saturday her potato peeler broke so Ellie went on to the laptop to buy a new one and while she was there she found herself in the kitchenware section and was amazed at what you could buy these days. A beeping kettle; whatever next, she thought to herself. Whatever next.

．

'Oh, that's new,' said Ellie's sister on her next visit.

Ellie looked at the new plaster goose sitting by the side of the log burner. 'Oh that silly thing, it's nothing,' she said.

'Not that,' said her sister. 'I meant the kettle.'

Ellie was filling up a shiny new Cuisinart kettle at the sink instead of the ancient old thing that used to sit on the gas hob.

'Does it beep?' asked her sister.

'What do you mean?'

'The kettle, it looks like one of those that beeps when it's about to boil. Does it beep?'

Ellie looked flustered. 'It does actually. It's very... convenient.'

'Did the old one start to leak?'

'No. No, it was just that I... Well, I'd had it a long time and, you know...'

'It was time for a new one. I get it. Well, it's good to see your getting on with the Internet. I take it you bought it online. Not been sneaking into town, have you?'

'Of course not. I can't, can I?'

The kettle beeped and Ellie blushed a little as she poured the boiling water over a couple of tea bags. Her sister saw the colour in her cheeks. 'Don't worry,' she said. 'Its nice to have a few nice things. You can afford to treat yourself from time to time. Just keep an eye on it, that 's my advice.'

Ellie squirmed at her younger sister's patronising tone but she said nothing and let the teabags dunk while she looked in the cupboard for the ginger biscuits.

'Have you bought anything else?' asked her sister.

'No,' and Ellie shook her head enough to make her bird's-nest hair wobble.

'What about that duck by the fire?'

'It's a goose.'

'Its new is what it is.'

'And it's lovely,' said Ellie.

Her sister smiled smugly. 'This was your idea, you know,' said Ellie, handing her a mug of tea and a biscuit.

.

Slowly, so slowly that at first she didn't notice a thing, Ellie's life began to change.

Ellie had lived in her little cottage for more than twenty years and most of the things that she had in it were not far off the same age. Ellie liked fixing things and Ellie liked making do. She didn't see that anything new was intrinsically better than anything that wasn't new. She liked things that lasted. She didn't like window-shopping; she didn't subscribe to a catalogue or anything like that. In fact, even the flyers that the postman left in her letterbox listing the offers in the local shops went straight into the recycling before she even read a single word. For Ellie, shopping was a necessary evil and all that she ever bought was what she referred to as "the necessaries".

Food.

Clothes.

Household cleaning stuff.

And now, all of a sudden, beeping kettles and Orla Kiely mugs.

It was a puzzle to Ellie as to how this change had come about, but it clearly had.

She would be sweeping the kitchen floor with a brush she had been using for years and every time she used it, every time its almost bald, bristle-less head swept the tiles, she would think to herself that it really was time to get a new one but then she did nothing about it. But now she just opened up the laptop and bought one. It was as simple as that. She knew that the following day Dwayne would be jogging down her drive with a new broom in a box. Her wish had not just come true; it had been delivered to her door.

Vitamins. Ellie believed in vitamins and she had a cupboard full of them. When she ran out of one before, she had always picked them up from the supermarket but now she didn't have to wait to add them to the weekly online shop; she could just get them from Amazon. Dwayne would park his big white van at the end of her drive and he would come jogging over with his huge smile and a tiny brown cardboard box that had an even smaller bottle of vitamins inside it. Ellie would feel a twinge of guilt when that happened – but she did it anyway.

And then there was the stuff that not only did she not really need, she hadn't even known it existed.

A heated butterknife.

A grape-slicer you could also use on cherry tomatoes.

A battery-operated scrubbing brush for the dishes.

A 20-piece lock picks set with transparent training padlock. Well, thought Ellie when she bought it, you never know when that might turn out to be a useful skill.

Quite often Ellie would be thinking about some little job that needed doing around the house and before she knew it, she had opened up the laptop and started searching online. That was how she came to own a 26-piece vegetable chopping set, her bleeping kettle and no fewer than three carpet sweepers. She had a Crock-Pot Slow Cooker, "For cooks who are always on the go", and a 1000-piece jigsaw for people with too much time on their hands. Dwayne was a daily visitor at Ellie's door.

The next time her sister sat down at the kitchen table

she noticed that she was drinking tea out of a new Orla Kiely mug.

'These are nice,' she said, holding up the mug.

Ellie smiled. 'They are, aren't they? You can get no end of things in the same sort of pattern. Everything to match,' and she laughed but her laugh sounded tired and it wouldn't fly.

'You're keeping an eye on your spending, are you? It can add up.'

'Oh, I've just bought a few bits and pieces. You said I should treat myself every now and then.'

'Well, as long as you don't get carried away.'

When it came time to leave, Ellie walked her sister to her car. As they passed the barn her sister looked at the double doors. 'They look as if they have been opened recently. You haven't been driving, have you?'

'How could I? You've got the keys, and what about that insurance thing? I'm not allowed, am I?' and Ellie bundled her sister into the BMW before anything more could be said.

Ellie walked back to the barn and looked around before tugging the doors open. Her little silver car was still in there but it was now half-buried under a pile of Amazon packaging. Most of the boxes had been torn open but some of them had not; they had just been flung into the garage and Ellie hadn't bothered to open them at all.

Ellie bit her lip and looked a little worried before she carefully closed the doors again and made sure that this time, they looked shut.

For the next few days the laptop stayed unopened and Ellie saw nothing of Dwayne. She tried to busy herself with jobs around the house but she found it hard to avoid the burning desire for feather dusters, microfiber cloths and hand-held vacuum cleaners. She knew they were all there, just a click away.

She went for walks in the woods but couldn't avoid feeling a heartfelt need for extra long wellie-boot socks and possibly one of those Nordic walking sticks.

When she tucked herself up in bed at night, her toes resting on the warm and cosy, cuddly goose-covered hot water bottle, she caught herself thinking that just one more Swarovski crystal goose on her bedside table would complete the set. Well, maybe two more.

.

'You work awful long hours,' said Ellie.

'Oh, I don't know,' replied Dwayne. 'Anyway, it's nice to get out and about. You know, stretch your legs and that.'

Dwayne was carrying four parcels; three little ones balanced on top of one big one. He was also, Ellie noticed, rocking a pair of gold hoop earrings. 'They are nice,' she said.

'Thank you, Mrs Bolitho,' said Dwayne. 'I saw them and just thought that they were very me,' and he smiled a pearly smile.

'Well, I think they suit you.'

'That's nice to know, Mrs Bolitho,' and he handed the parcels over.

Ellie looked at them and wondered what on earth they could be.

.

In the morning, she sat in the kitchen hugging her mug of tea until it went cold, her eyes fixed on the laptop. It sat there, lifeless and inert, but there was something about it that pulled at her attention. It seemed to want to be turned on. Perhaps if she browsed now she might see that one thing that she absolutely positively needed – whatever it turned out to be. It promised to fulfil all her wishes, even the ones she didn't know she had. Just one little click and then it was just a matter of waiting for Dwayne to ring the doorbell.

A pair of cats came into the kitchen and started meowing for food. Ellie pulled open one of the kitchen cabinets and an avalanche of brown cardboard spilled out onto the floor. The cats turned tail and ran leaving the higgledy-piggledy Amazon logos grinning up at Ellie.

She tried to laugh, but somehow it didn't seem funny.

·

Ellie was used to living on a tight budget, being careful with her money, and so she had her bank send quarterly statements. They didn't like doing it, but they found that according to their own small print, they didn't have any choice.

The postman brought the statement along with a special-offer flyer from the Londis in the village and a new-deals circular from the household goods shop in town. Both the leaflets were consigned to the recycling on arrival leaving the statement to sit inside its envelope on the kitchen table.

Ellie wasn't sure she wanted to open it.

She pushed it around on the tabletop with the tip of her finger, as if she was moving a chess piece in a game she didn't think she would win.

At last she got the letter opener out of the drawer where it lived. It was a very nice letter opener and quite new. It had a handle in the shape of a goose.

Ellie slit the envelope open and pulled out the statement.

It gave her the surprise of her life.

·

Ellie's sister was due to visit the following day and sure enough, at about half-past three, Ellie saw the black BMW come slowly down the lane. The puddles had all dried up but the potholes were still there. Ellie's sister parked beside the barn. The geese waddled up and hissed at her. The cats looked on with disinterest. The kettle beeped.

The sisters sat at the kitchen table with Orla Kiely mugs of tea and biscuits on matching plates. There was a new tablecloth and a new vase filled with cut flowers. The laptop was closed and pushed over towards the window, out of their way.

Ellie's sister began with the usual gossip and news; tittle-tattle about people she worked with, chit-chat about her neighbours. Ellie listened and nodded and made the right noises and poured more tea. Ellie only had one piece of news and she didn't think she wanted to tell her sister that.

'A funny thing happened the other day,' said her sister. 'I bumped into the young man who sold us...' and she nodded at the laptop. 'That.'

'Oh really? Well he does work in town so it's not that odd, is it.'

'Well, no. Of course not, but it was the way he behaved that was funny. Downright odd, I would call it.'

Ellie raised her eyebrows.

'I was in town. Just on my way to Marks when there he was. He grabbed me outside Greggs. It was most peculiar, I can tell you.'

Ellie pursed her lips.

'He went on and on like a mad thing. Said that he shouldn't have sold us the laptop and please could he have it back. I said no, of course. I mean, the very idea.'

Ellie nodded in agreement.

'He said his boss was furious. He said he'd pay twice what we paid for it. Well, I don't like being told what to do, as you well know,' Ellie nodded. 'And I could see no reason why we'd sell it back to him as we had bought it in good faith.'

Ellie nodded more emphatically.

'Then he touched me. He laid hands on me. Can you believe it? I was shocked.'

Ellie's eyes grew large.

'I told him that I was calling the police unless he went away and left me alone right that very instant.'

'Quite right too,' said Ellie.

'He let go of my arm but he was still standing right in front of me. Then, well, you'll never guess what.'

'What?'

'He said I could name my price.'

'I bet he did.'

'What do you mean?'

Ellie frowned for a moment. 'Nothing. Well, it just sounds like the sort of thing he would have said. Did you tell him it wasn't yours to sell?' asked Ellie.

'He stopped me in the street, Ellie,' said her sister shaking her head. 'I only did what I thought was right.'

'Of course you did,' said Ellie. 'Did you tell him it was mine?'

'We were outside Greggs,' said he sister. 'We were in the street outside Greggs.'

After her sister had left, Ellie sat quietly for a time piecing the bits of the story together.

A cat jumped up on her lap and she stroked it while she thought about what she knew. She made herself a fresh mug of tea. She always thought better after a nice mug of tea. She fished the bank statement out of the kitchen drawer, opened it and read it again although she knew very well what it said. Other than a few direct debits to pay the household bills, no money had left her account at all and no payments had been charged to her card.

Everything that Dwayne had delivered over the past six or more weeks had been free.

Ellie had paid for none of it.

Ellie wondered why that might have happened.

It might have been her nephew, she thought. He had set everything up for her on the laptop; he had set up all the accounts with Amazon and Tesco and the others. Had he done something wrong, or was he one of these Slashers, or Hitchers or whatever they called themselves who broke into websites to steal information – or just to steal? Was he a hacker? That was it thought Ellie. That's what they were called. But why would he do it? He was her nephew but they weren't that close. it wasn't a favour for a beloved Aunt.

Ellie blew on her tea to cool it.

And now Ellie had this new part of the story that she had been told today. The man from the shop would certainly want the laptop back if it could be used to buy stuff without paying for it. It would make perfect sense to say that they could name their price. If there was something about the laptop that made every bit of Internet shopping free then the computer was priceless.

Ellie took a sip of tea.

It was hard to believe that technology like that would be in a second-hand laptop sitting in a junkshop window. It just didn't seem terribly likely to Ellie. Not that she knew much about technology, but all the same…

There was one more possibility that she could think of.

She could think it, but could she possibly believe it?

She took her mug over to the sink and put it with the washing up.

Ellie realised there was a story floating in the corner of her mind, something from her childhood. A story she used to read to her sister when she was young and Ellie was doing the looking after. It was one of their favourites. It was a story about a character that someone had recently reminded her of.

Ah yes, thought Ellie at last, it was obvious now.

She should have seen it before.

Ellie set the laptop down on the table in front of her. She checked to see that it was turned off and that the Ethernet cable wasn't attached.

She looked at it for a long minute before touching the closed machine with the tip of one finger. There was just the slightest tingle of static electricity. The sensation became stronger as she stroked her finger across the metal case.

How did you do this, she thought, how are you supposed to rub the lamp? Use a silk square or microfiber cloth? She couldn't remember what the story had said; it had been a long time ago.

'I think you just rub with your fingers,' said Ellie to one of her cats. The cat arched its back and hissed before dashing out of the door.

Ellie shrugged and used the pads of her fingers to rub the laptop; back and forth, back and forth.

Through the kitchen window Ellie saw a zephyr swirl across the lawn and gather up the russet leaves. As it became stronger the tops of the trees along the lane bowed their heads like courtiers. Ellie could hear the roar of the wind now. The hens ran for the hen house, the geese hissed from the banks of the stream and the cats were nowhere to be seen. On the table the laptop was still closed but a glow escaped from beneath its lid as if the screen was burning bright. Ellie pushed her chair back. The kitchen windows rattled in their frames. Out on the drive sticks and even some small branches joined the leaves in a whirlwind, a tornado moving towards Ellie's cottage. Ellie clapped her hands to her face and peered through the window. The twister sounded as if it had made its way to the kitchen door and then the door banged open and the wind threw branches and leaves over the threshold and into the kitchen. With a suddenness that frightened Ellie almost as much as anything that had gone before it, the wind stopped, the vortex dropped all that it had collected on its rundown the drive with a clatter and all was silent.

Then came a familiar voice. 'Your wish is my command, Mrs Bolitho.'

Ellie laughed in delight. Her laughter fluttered around the room like a songbird released from a gilded cage.

.

'At last, ' said Dwayne. 'I was beginning to think you'd never let me out,' and he scowled at the laptop sitting on the kitchen table.

'Cramped is it?' asked Ellie.

'Its enough to make your toes curl,' muttered Dwayne.

Ellie looked at Dwayne. Dwayne the D'jini as he now was. He was fatter and bluer and his curly-toed shoes were floating just above the ground. His polyester jumper had become a silken waistcoat. His combat trousers were billowing pantaloons. His beard was pointier. His ponytail had become a topknot. He had kohl around his eyes and henna tattoos on the backs of his hands. Dwayne the D'jini. The deliverer of wishes.

'Shouldn't you be in a lamp?' asked Ellie

'You have to move with the times, Mrs Bolitho,' he replied.

'But why a computer?'

'The choice isn't down to me. That isn't how it works, but they are what people wish on these days, Mrs Bolitho. They are where people keep their dreams, where they actually list their wishes.'

Ellie nodded. 'Perhaps they do. People say they believe in technology, don't they?'

'Yes, they do, and I think all that means is that people don't believe in anything anymore.'

'So do I get three wishes?' she asked.

'You've gone well past your three already haven't you, Mrs Bolitho?' said Dwayne looking at the Cuisinart kettle and the Orla Kiely mugs and all the rest of it. 'Anyway, having just three wishes seems rather out of step with today's world, don't you think? I think people expect rather more than that. Bonus wishes and added wishes and extra wishes. Doesn't that sound rather more like what people expect?'

'Say it again,' said Ellie suddenly grinning from ear to ear.

Dwayne frowned. 'Your wish is my command,' he said rather reluctantly.

Ellie laughed and clapped her hands like a little girl being told a particularly good story.

'Then can I have world peace and an end to starvation and governments that are more inclusive and look after the needs of the vulnerable and disenfranchised?'

Dwayne gritted his teeth and sunk his neck into his shoulders. 'No. No I can't do that. What about something more along the lines of a 64-piece bone china dinner service or I can do you the latest smart phone with 108mega pixel camera in a rose-gold case. It's very nice.'

Ellie shook her head. 'So you can't make my wishes come true then. I think I may as well put you back in the …' and she nodded towards the laptop on the kitchen table. It looked rather small compared to Dwayne. He scowled and folded his arms across his chest. 'You were happy enough with all the shopping,' said Dwayne and Ellie had to admit that was true.

'What about your weight in jewels, I can do that.'

'Are you trying to be funny,' said Ellie looking down at her waistline.

'This used to be much easier,' grumbled Dwayne.

'Perhaps we are just spoiled for choice.'

Dwayne pondered for a moment. He twisted the strands of his pointy beard in his fingers. He chewed his lip. Suddenly he popped a finger in the air and wagged it, knowingly. 'What about travel?' he said. 'What about exploring the mystic Orient? What about wandering through the dusty souks of Arabia?'

Ellie smiled at the idea. She had never been past the Tamar before.

'Flying carpet?' she asked.

'No. But I can do you a Business Class ticket on Emirates,' and Ellie laughed out loud.

.

The next time that Ellie's sister came to visit she had it in mind to see if she could persuade Ellie to sell back the laptop after all. When she came to think about it, 'Name your price' sounded like rather a lot of money. But when she arrived at Ellie's cottage she discovered that it was all locked up and Ellie was nowhere to be seen.

**SIMON MINCHIN**

# TOPPLE

RODGER CAME down into the kitchen and saw that the percolator was already on. The room smelt of wood-smoke and coffee. It was warm and deeply reassuring. He shuffled across the kitchen floor to pour himself a mug.

'Morning, Da,' said Precious.

'Hey, you. How's the little horror?'

Precious was sitting on the hearth blowing life back into the coals. Swaddled on her hip was a little bundle with a relatively new life in it.

'He's fine Da. I've just fed him so if you're quiet he'll go off.'

'Let me hold him.'

'He's almost asleep. Leave him be.'

'Oh, go on.'

Precious smiled up at her father. Her almond eyes crinkled and dimples appeared in her coffee-coloured cheeks. 'Try not to wake him, please.'

Rodger crossed the kitchen floor as quietly as a draft. He took the bundle from his daughter's hip. His hands were big and raw-boned with pink calloused palms. He lifted the bundle ever so gently. It was hard to believe that these hands could be so tender. His grandson had tightly closed eyes and a furiously pursed mouth; that ancient anger that all new-borns seem to feel: fury about all the things that had been done to the world before they had a chance to say yes or no. Rodger lifted the bundle higher and higher until the child was raised above his head, and then there was a hiccup and a gurgle.

'Give him here, Da. He needs burping.'

'I just wanted to show him to the gods,' he said. 'Let them know he's fam. You know, one of us.'

'He looks like his dad.'

'He so does not. I never understand why people say that anyway. All babies look like sea monsters but people are always saying, oh-he-looks-just-like-his-dad. No. They never do. Who is his father anyway?'

'Some lucky boy,' and Precious nuzzled her baby, nose to nose. 'You don't look like a monster, do you?' she cooed.

Rodger sat down on the hearth next to his daughter. He leant in towards the embers and blew one long, gentle breath. A flame flickered into life. 'I've got the knack, you see,' and Precious chuckled at that. She rested her head on her father's shoulder and tucked the baby in to her oxter.

'Do you want more coffee?' she asked.

'In a minute. It's nice just sitting here.'

'What are you doing today?'

Rodger chewed at his lip and scratched the stubble on his chin. 'This and that. I'll check on the flock and get a couple of lambs for the table. I'd like to get another Glasshouse wall planted.'

'You taking Josh with you?'

'I thought I would. Give me a chance to um…'

'You won't change his mind you know. He's set on it.'

Rodger used a scrap of firewood to pick at his teeth. He fidgeted and avoided Precious' gaze. 'I know, but I wish he wasn't.'

'You got to let him have his head, make him own mistakes, if that's what happens.'

'Problem with mistakes is that they don't just affect them that make 'em, do they?'

The three of them sat quietly for a few moments while the fire grew back to life. There was a buzzing noise and Rodger pulled his tablet from a pocket. 'I gotta go,' he said reading the screen. 'Give me a hug.'

Precious very gently sat her baby down on the kitchen floor. She balanced him. The swaddling let her set him upright. His eyes were half closed and he blew a milky bubble from his lips.

'Have you got a name for him yet?' asked Rodger.

'No. I'm still thinking about it. I got to find what suits him.' And as they watched, the bundle of swaddling began to sway and then slowly and gently fell over onto one side. The little pink face sticking out of the top blinked in mild surprise and then he looked around, fascinated by his new perspective on the world. Precious scooped her son back up into her arms. 'Have a good day,' she said and the nameless child gurgled his agreement.

·

The Tang Clanhouse was a massive redbrick block that sat half-crumbled on the edge of the Lundun river. It had lost part of its roof and one of the four cream spires had collapsed and fallen. The riverside curtain wall had been taken down by the first Tangs to live here and the enormous inner hall was now where the Stiltwalkers for the rice fields were kept and the pads for the BEEs, the rest of the building was a rabbit warren of halls and galleries, balconies and corridors that connected sleeping quarters and social spaces with silos and stores for everything the clan grew. It was a mystery as to what it had originally been built for. Rodger thought it had probably been a temple because of the spires but it was just the Tang House in Battersee now, halfway between the Sitee and Shellsea.

On the way to the BEE, Rodger picked up a pair of workhounds from their kennels. They followed him with the strange, half-sinuous, half-jerky way they had of moving. Their servos hissed and clicked as they trotted at his heels. He tried to raise his son on his tablet but eventually gave up and left a voice message. 'Hi, Josh. I'm on my way to the BEE now. Meet you there, OK?'

Farmboys were opening the hall doors that led out onto the river. Three Stiltwalkers stood in a line waiting to stride out of the hall and begin tending the rice paddies. Rodger recognised Alyssa strapped into the nearest walker. He waved and walked over to say hello. Alyssa dropped the control seat of the walker down to its lowest level. The walker's gyros grumbled as they kept it balanced on the hard hall floor.

'First shift,' he said when she was close enough to hear him above the whine of the walker's motors.

'Yeah. I like to get it done.'

'And then you got the rest of the day to play with your new cuz, eh?'

Alyssa squeaked. 'But he's so cute,' she squealed. 'He looks just like…'

'Don't,' said Rodger. 'Just don't say it.'

The hall doors swung fully back and Rodger and Alyssa peered out into the new day. The sun was weak and watery. A pale mist hung over the paddy fields.

'It'll burn off. The forecast is good. You'll need a hat by mid-shift.'

'All I've got to do is plant out these plugs and then a couple of hours in the nursery beds. Where are you off to?'

'Check on the Flyover Fields first off then… Oh, looks like you're off.' The first Stiltwalker was moving, the three long, tapering legs clicking over the hall floor. The gyros spooled up and their hum changed pitch as they kept the walker balanced. The pilot had the platform at the highest setting but when they were working it would slide down the articulated legs until it was just above the water level.

For killoms either side of the Tang House the great Lundun river had been partially drained and damned and the Tangs had made the resultant mud flats into the most productive rice fields in Urope.

'Precious told me, if I saw you, to tell you to take it easy on Josh, yeah?'

Rodger shook his head in disbelief. 'I just want to talk to…'

Alyssa smoothed one hand over her shaved scalp and waved the other at her father. She grinned. 'See what we mean, eh?' Her bright eyes sparkled against her black skin as she laughed. 'Do you see what we mean? You need to listen, not talk.' and she set the platform to its top position and Rodger heard her laughter fade as she slid smoothly up into the air.

'Who would have daughters, man?' he mumbled to himself as he walked towards the pad.

Josh was already there, helping the farmboys swing the rolls of mesh into the BEE's cargo pod and sliding the stock container in behind them. The power loader had dropped the container a few centimetres short and Josh was trying to manhandle it into position.

'Watch your fingers,' shouted Rodger and Josh turned around, an exasperated look on his face. 'I know. I know. I can look after myself.'

'You're only fifteen…'

'Almost seventeen.'

'Whatever. A farm is a dangerous place. That thing will take a finger off without blinking.'

'I know, Dad. You told us. You told us every single day and yet…' and Josh held up his hands and waggled their full compliment of digits.

Rodger shook his head in frustration. His short dreads bounced from side to side. He walked towards his eldest son. It felt like he had a thousand words in his head, all of them struggling to be the first ones spoken and yet, to his own surprise, the ones that first came out were, 'Cheeky twat.'

.

The BEE's yellow nose cone had a pair of tinted blister-windows set into it like bug's eyes. Behind each of the windows was a control seat; high-backed and skeletally ergonomic, like a neoprene-covered spine. The six wings and the battery packs for the motivators were attached to the middle of the BEE. The rear section was one big cylindrical cargo pod painted with broad yellow and black stripes. The whole thing sat on three pairs of hydraulic legs. Two remote grapples were slung under the cockpit and a pair of antenna protruded from the top.

'Who's driving?' asked Rodger.

'You can. It might stop you nagging me.'

Rodger whistled and the two workhounds jerked awake. He whistled again, a long quavering note that changed pitch and ended in a series of pulses. The workhounds decoded the whistle and then leapt into the stock container where they settled down on the floor. Josh and Rodger climbed the crew access steps and then swung themselves into the skeletal chairs.

'Wing check?'

'Should do, I suppose.'

Rodger tapped the control screen and a warning buzzer sounded as the wings cycled up. Josh checked the camera screens. It looked like the farmboys had backed off far enough and he nodded at his father. Rodger took manual control of each wing and put it through a cycle. First of all it slowly unfurled, then took a downbeat before returning to their hold position.

'Number 3's got a static build up,' said Josh.

'There's nothing on the board.' Rodger frowned at the warning lights that were showing green for each wing.

'It's not much, but I can hear it.'

'Is it the muscle pack or the actuator?'

'Dunno. It'll be fine, anyway. Let's go.'

Rodger's hands floated over the screen again. The tinted cupolas closed over their seats. The wings beat faster and faster until the BEE lifted gently off the deck. Its hydraulic legs folded up and bounced gently as they locked in place. It hovered, swaying from side to side. The flight computer calibrated itself.

'You know that theoretically, these things can't fly, don't you?' said Josh.

'Yep. I do.' Rodger flicked the thumb-stick, stamped on the lift pedal and the BEE shot forward and climbed fast. It swerved out of the hall bay doors missing Alyssa's Stiltwalker by barely a couple of metres before soaring up into the misty sky. In the rear-view camera screen they could both see Alyssa giving them the finger.

'What happened to farms being dangerous places and always staying safe?' grumbled Josh.

'Missed her by killoms,' laughed his father.

The BEE climbed and climbed until Rodger slowed the rate of ascent and settled into hover mode. They were a good way up. It felt as if they could see from one side of Lundun to the other; a broken landscape of shattered brick and stone, architecture that was becoming geology. The old river was a flat silver ribbon that swayed through the tumbled building blocks of the broken city. The metropolis had crumbled into a mosaic of red, yellow and grey slabs, interlocked and fitting tightly together. Off towards the east, they could just make out the towering shapes of the Glasshouses. Further out past them were the docks and ponds of Canaree, where the Enders Clan had their beds and hatcheries.

'Beautiful, isn't it?' murmured Rodger. 'This is our home. This is where we're meant to live. Man has always been a city dweller. It's natural for us. It's how the gods intended it to be.'

'But there's a big wide world out there as well.'

'What, beyond the Orbital? That's just poisoned earth. No place for us.'

'I know. I know. I'm not talking about the Cunty but there are other cities in Urope. They might be worth a visit.'

'Is that why you want to ship out on the Tinker?'

'It would be good experience.'

'You think? There might be good experiences for you here?'

'It's not just about the travel. It's about what I might learn.' Josh waved a hand at the city beneath them. 'I'd love to see us take all this back. For the whole city to be filled with people again.'

Angrily Rodger twisted the throttle and the increased wing beats drowned the possibility of any more words. Josh pursed his lips and stared out of the blister window as the empty cityscape slid beneath them.

.

Tang Clan grazed their sheep on sections of the old flyovers, the massive raised slabs that the ancients had built for their ground cars.

When the first Tangs had started changing the river into a series of rice paddies, one of them had had the bright idea of spraying the dredged silt mixed with grass seed on to the flyovers where it quickly established a layer of fertile topsoil that grew into rich pasture. Raised on concrete stilts above the broken canyons of ruined buildings, the flyovers were already walled and linked together so when the flocks had cropped one section it was easy work to drive them along to the next. The sheep were safe and appeared to enjoy being on higher ground, above the Lundun fogs and mists.

'Remind me again what we are doing?' said Josh.

'There are a couple of farmboys staying out with this

flock, see?' Rodger pointed to a big shipping container over by the flyover wall. 'That's their shepherd-hut. I've messaged them so they'll be here in a minute. I want to pick up a couple of lambs for home and then we'll take the boys down to Sitee and they can get on with a couple of jobs down there.'

'Are we doing that with them? I'm not wild about working at those heights.'

'No. There's something down there that I want to show you.'

'Oh, good,' said Josh sounding relieved.

Rodger swung the BEE up over the wall that edged the flyover and let it settle on the grass. The comms buzzed and Rodger tapped his earpiece. 'OK, see you in a bit,' he said to the dashboard mic then his hands floated over the controls. The wings furled into their carry position, the legs folded down until the rear of the cargo pod touched the grass and then Rodger shut the BEE down. They sat in silence for a moment, each with their own thoughts. Rodger looked at his eldest son; he was supposed to be listening to Josh but the boy wasn't saying anything.

'I s'pose I wanted to get out from under my father when I was your age,' Rodger said quietly dipping a toe in the water.

'Don't make this all about you,' said Josh. 'It's not about you or Mother or anyone but me. I want to see the world. I want to explore. Discover new things. Make a difference.'

'You can make a difference here.'

'Oh, come on. Nothing ever changes here. Nothing ever will.'

'What?'

'What's changed since you became head of the Clan?'

Rodger looked shocked. 'We grow more rice, more squash, more soya, more…'

'Exactly. It's just more of the same and not even much more of that.'

'The Glasshouses are down to me.'

'A good idea, but only one idea, and it hasn't changed the world, has it?'

Rodger kept his jaw clamped tight.

'So we grow a bit more, and even that's mostly because of this stuff.' Josh tapped the dashboard in front of him. 'It's down to the tech that we buy, Tinker-built stuff like the Stiltwalkers, the workhounds and this BEE. We are getting to be better farmers but only because the Tinkers are becoming better engineers. No other reason.'

Rodger pursed his lips. 'We grow all the food we need. No one in Urope goes hungry anymore.'

'True. But how many people are there? Not so many. If we want to feed more people we need to learn what the ancients did, how they did things before the dark times.'

'No,' barked his father 'Not that. Never like that again.'

Josh sighed. 'How many people live in Lundun?' he asked.

Rodger rubbed his chin and scowled. 'A lot. Some of the other Clans are bigger than us…'

'How many? Roughly.'

'Six or seven hundred? Perhaps a thousand. That's hard to believe, I know but…'

'It used to be ten million.'

Rodger laughed. 'You don't believe those old stories, do you?'

'It's true.'

'And if it was true, do you think life was any better?'

Josh turned away angrily. His mouth was a thin, indignant line. He glowered out of the blister window at the two farmboys arriving on their quad. He could feel his father's eyes drilling in to the back of his head.

'I want to help build our world back to what it was,' said Josh. His breath steamed the plexiglass bubble. 'Would that be so bad?'

.

The workhounds appeared to bound about like playful puppies but they were scanning the terrain and plotting where the sheep were. They used algorithms to predict the flock behaviour so that they could herd them. Josh joked with the young farmboys. Rodger stood by the flyover wall, arms folded, looking out over Lundun.

'What about these two?' shouted Josh pointing at a pair of fat yearlings the hounds had cut from the flock.

'I don't mind,' replied his father without turning round. 'You choose.'

'What matter wiv Boss Man?' said one of the farmboys under his breath.

'Oh.' Josh wrinkled his lip. 'I think I've pissed him off.'

'Dat a boy's job,' said the farmboy, grinning through the mess of tattoos that covered his face. 'My old man fuckin' hate me.' He laughed out loud and clapped Josh on the back. 'You doin' good, Little Boss. How you upset him?'

'I don't want to be a farmer just yet.'

'Whaaaa…'

'Well, thing is, I want to join the Tinkers for a season or two. I'm good with tech. It's what I enjoy. But…'

'You tellin' 'im that but what he hear is you sayin' no

to the farmin'. What he hear is you sayin' no to him and
him life.'

Josh nodded. 'Yep. All that and more, believe me.'

The farmboy sighed. He flicked the piercing in his lip
with the tip of his tongue. 'Dat a ting, Little Boss. You just
gotta talk it out, you know. You both fam and fam come
together in the end. Dat's how it is.'

Josh smiled. 'Perhaps you're right,' he said, looking
around for his father. 'But we're not having much luck
today.'

There was a piercing whistle. Josh looked for the
workhounds but they were in the back of the BEE. His
father stuck his head out of the cockpit window and raised
his eyebrows in question.

'He's whistling for me, isn't he?' growled Josh under his
breath. 'He's fuckin' whistling for me.'

.

Rodger took the BEE straight up into the clear, blue sky.
The airframe trembled as he wound more power into the
wings. Father and son concentrated very hard on not
looking at each other; Josh stared at his tablet, Rodger
studied the controls. He let the BEE roll and yaw into a
sweeping turn. There were muffled yells from the back.

'We got passengers, remember,' muttered Josh. Rodger
grunted and settled the BEE back on to the straight and
level.

'I thought we were going to Sitee,' said Josh. 'This is the
wrong way.'

'I want to show you something first.'

'Oh right. What?'

'You'll see.'

They had passed over the crackled mosaic of Lundun town now and were out above the rough; the abandoned scrub and waste land that was the buffer zone between where men lived and where the Orbital acted as a barrier against the horror of the Cunty on the other side.

'I told your sisters that I wouldn't do all the talking. That I'd listen to you,' said Rodger at last. 'That only works if you do some talking, doesn't it.'

Josh pursed his lips and screwed up his eyes. He let a long deep breath out but still said nothing.

'You can say anything. Anything you want,' Rodger frowned. 'We used to get on. We used to have fun.'

'That was when I was a boy, before I grew up.'

'Who says you're grown up now?'

Josh turned in his seat and growled. 'Who says you are?'

Rodger clenched his jaw then dropped the nose of the BEE and nodded towards what was appearing out of the haze.

'Over there. Look.'

Ahead of them was the twisting, sinuous silver ribbon that was the Orbital. 50 metres wide, it circled Lundun like a necklace. Every few killoms other bands of concrete and steel were woven into it making the shapes of ancient knots; patterns impossible to recognise on the ground, they could only be seen from the air. The Orbital had stopped the devastation that had destroyed England's landscape. The Orbital had left Lundun safe and sound. Rodger dropped the BEE down towards a pattern in the ribbon where broad, silvery lines drew leaf-shaped blades across the landscape.

'Let me guess,' said Josh. 'You are going to show me

how much worse the world is outside Lundun so I should just stay home with the fam.'

'No. I'm going to tell you…' Rodger shrugged. 'Oh, I don't know. Maybe you're right. Thing is, I want you to make your own decisions but I want to help you make the right ones, if that makes any sense.'

'Yeah. I know.' Josh smiled. 'But…'

'But?'

'But I don't want my life to be a rewind of yours.'

Rodger nodded. 'I get that. It's just this whole tech thing, it's hard for me to like.' He slowed the BEE down until they were hovering above the leaf pattern in the Orbital. 'I mean, just look,' said Rodger and he gestured at the ground beneath them. The landscape was devastated. The land itself was dead, a vast featureless plain of mud and run-off water. It was a panorama of nothing but slurry decorated here and there with floating concrete slabs that supported the rusty iron skeletons of ancient barns and cattle sheds, but nothing could graze here now and most probably never would.

'This is what you get when you let tech-heads farm,' said Rodger. 'They followed the science. They soaked the ground in chemz and fertilizer. The cattle were fed on steroids and the ground-up carcasses of their own dead.'

'We know better now.'

'Farmers do, but farmers always did.'

'We all know better.'

'And we can all forget so quickly.'

In the water and on the mud were sickly green nitrogen blooms that looked diseased and disgusting. The land was painted in the colours of the chemicals that had been sprayed on it. A lab experiment run wild on a countrywide scale.

'Do you know why they did this? To grow enough food to feed your ten million or however many it was. All those mouths. Look what it took to feed them, and in the end, they couldn't even do that.' Rodger let them roll into a long shallow curve out over the polluted land and then back over the Orbital once again.

'But it doesn't have to be that way,' said Josh.

'No, it doesn't. We farm the clan way. We follow nature's rules and nature's laws, and so we lead a good life. A life that will still be here when Precious's baby is as old as you are now.'

'We can have both.'

'No, I don't think we can. I really don't,' said Rodger. The wings changed pitch and began to beat faster. The BEE flew away from the Orbital and towards the glass towers of the Sitee.

.

The Tang Clan were known for the Flyover Fields and the rice paddies in the silt of the Lundun river, but what really defined them were the Glasshouses. Years ago the centre of Lundun, the Sitee, was a collection of tall glass towers, devoid of life and empty of purpose. Three or four hundred meters tall they came in all shapes and forms; straight edged and geometric, curving and organic. What was common to them all was their height and the fact that they were all clad in glass. The Glasshouses glinted in the dawn and glowed ruby-red in the evening light. At the time, the farming clans were all growing and trying new things. The Enders had re-worked the old docks and water-treatment works out in the East of Lundun to grow shrimp, conger and spirulina. The Khan Clan were opening up the labyrinth of tunnels beneath Lundun's streets. The tunnels provided moisture and a stable temperature and once the Khans built mirrored light traps to funnel sunlight underground they started to produce root vegetables, fungi and mushrooms as well as yeast and moulds that were processed into protein blocks. Clan Hood fenced off a great park that had been one of Lundun's green spaces and farmed deer and llama there but it was a slow and inefficient process. Many of the other clans had their own projects, some a success and some not.

Meanwhile, Clan Tang sat and watched. A young Rodger sat and watched.

Now, years later, Rodger watched as the Glasshouses came closer and closer. They all had their own names now; the Box, the Knife, the Shard, the Slice, the Egg and all the others. About half of them were producing food but Clan Tang had its stamp on all of them. The Sitee was Tang territory.

'That planting mesh is coming loose,' said Josh pointing at the nearest Glasshouse.

'We'll get the farmboys to look at it,' muttered Rodger. 'They can do it after they've hung the new mats. I want to show you the inside. You've never been inside, have you.'

Josh nodded. 'No, I haven't. I didn't think anyone had.'

Rodger didn't reply.

The Glasshouses were disappearing under hanging curtains of green. From out here it looked as if the buildings were going mouldy, a little closer and they could see the vertical fields, the planting mats that were suspended from the tops of the towers and draped down the sides. Josh couldn't make out what was actually growing but it was probably kale and squash, sorghum and soya. The plants grew around each other tangling themselves into a dense carpet of supportive vegetation. The trick, the Clan had discovered, was to mix crops that would work together; the tendrils and vines of the squash added to the support that the planting mat provided, the heavy stems of the kale could take the buffeting of the wind and shelter the soya.

'It's like we picked up the fields and stuck them up in the sky,' said Josh. 'I bet it wasn't easy.'

They approached the tower and Rodger slowed the BEE down to a crawl. He slipped it into hover-mode when they were just twenty meters out. The kale and the big leaves on the squash flapped in the draft from the BEE's beating wings. They put down on the Glasshouse roof. Josh and Rodger helped the farmboys with their safety harnesses.

'Dis my most un-favourite job, man,' said one of them. 'Farmin' a t'ing you should do with both feet on the ground.'

'We'll be back in an hour or so,' said Rodger and he led Josh over towards a stairhead that stood proud from the rest of the roof. He pressed a number sequence on the keypad next to the door and when it swung open he ushered Josh in.

Their work boots clanged on the metal treads and the echoes of their footsteps made the stairwell sound cavernous and cold. The stairwell sank down and down into the building like a vortex. For a minute or two Josh was envious of the farmboys hanging on to the outside of the building and swaying in the breeze. 'Don't worry,' said Rodger. 'I don't like it either but we're only going down a couple of floors. There's something I want you to see.'

'Been a day for sight seeing.'

'Well, if you're big enough to make decisions about your future you're old enough to know something about your past,' and they carried on spiralling down and down and down their footsteps sounding like tolling bells.

At last they stopped on a landing. Rodger pushed a fire door open and they stepped out on to a gantry in the middle of a huge space. Gangways and gantries spread like spiderweb amoungst massive tanks and rusty machines. Pipes flowed everywhere, some bigger than a man could stretch his arms around, some just the thickness of a finger. These were the veins, arteries and nerves of a body made of metal and plastic. Josh stared, wide eyed.

'These top floors are deeper than the others. The machinery for the lifts and the air handling is up here and there are those tanks. I think they were for a fire control system.'

'How do you mean?'

'Thousands of litres of water that could drench every floor in the Glasshouse.'

Rodger led Josh back out to the stairwell and down half a dozen more flights. The floor they came to was filled with racks. From floor to ceiling and from one side to the other, the space was filled with racked shelving and on that shelving were hundreds and thousands of trays connected with microbore pipework. There were the remains of hanging grow lamps and the cannibalised ductwork of the building's old air-handling system. Ladders led up to the top level of each rack and there were wheeled bins that had obviously been intended for collecting the harvest but the bins were empty. Every single growing tray on every single rack was thick with vegetation but every single plant was dead and had been for a very, very long time. The entire floor was absolutely full of dead plants.

'Every other floor is the same,' said Rodger. 'I think there are fifteen in the building.'

'Everything is dead?'

'Everything.'

'What happened?'

'We came to our senses,' said Rodger.

By the time they made it back up to the roof, the farmboys had finished their work and were sitting in the shelter of the BEE. Rodger hustled them into the cargo pod and within minutes they were airborne. Josh was staring out into the middle distance. 'How did you know that was there?' he said quietly. 'You knew the code to the door. You knew how it all worked. We all knew that growing mats on the Glasshouses was your idea but that wasn't the only idea you had, was it?' He turned to look at his father. 'Was it?'

Rodger concentrated on his flying and didn't reply.

Josh frowned and turned further towards his father.

'Those plants were growing without soil. They were growing without sunlight.' Josh's smooth brow was ploughed with frown lines. 'They would have grown all day and all night. They would have grown all summer and all through the winter.'

Rodger said nothing.

'That's a massive amount of food. Why did they die? Why did we stop?' Josh clenched his hands into fists. 'Talk to me,' he shouted.

'I thought I was supposed to be listening.'

Josh growled in frustration.

Lundun slid by underneath them, the vast urban landscape almost devoid of human life; just a few farms here and there like isolated villages living quietly in the depths of an enormous concrete forest.

'We could have taken all this back,' muttered Josh looking out over the city. 'We could have filled it with people.'

'Brilliant,' barked Rodger. 'Yeah, we could have started walking down exactly the same road that led us into darkness the first time. Why can't you see that?'

'You're just scared, old man. You're scared of progress.'

'You're fucking right I am. I've seen what progress looks like. We flew over it this morning, remember?'

Josh seemed about to spit back a reply but stopped himself. He sank his head into his hands. 'I'm sorry,' he said almost too quietly to be heard above the noise of the BEE. 'Just tell me what happened.'

Rodger thought for a moment and then said, 'I wasn't much older than you are now. Like you, I knew I was going to become head of the clan and, I guess like you, I wanted to do something special, to achieve something before the clan took over my life.'

Josh grunted in surprise.

'Those glass towers, I saw them everyday and I knew something about how the ancients used to use glass houses to grow more. They were built on the ground but still, you know, there was an idea there.'

Josh nodded. 'Yeah, I see that.'

'I thought they could be like the Flyover Fields or what the Enders were doing with the docks and we did with the river. Using something in a different way to grow stuff. To make the best of what there was. One day I was looking at the towers and I just saw them as vertical fields.'

'The idea just came to you, just like that?'

'But making it real, that was the problem.'

'I bet,' said Josh.

'Yeah. To do that I had to run away to the Tinker,' and Rodger grinned.

Josh's jaw sagged open.

The BEE floated on. The sun was dropping in the sky and the shadows were getting longer. The paddy fields were glowing a soft rose and the first murmuration of Lundun's starlings rose into the air and started to swirl into a liquid, three-dimensional dance.

Rodger looked at Josh's expression and laughed out loud.

'I don't believe it,' muttered Josh.

'Well,' said Rodger. 'Where do you think you got it from? The apple doesn't fall far from the tree, does it?'

'But you were so against me going to them.'

'Yes well, my experience didn't turn out so good so…'

'Tell me,' said Josh.

Rodger eased back on the power until the BEE was just bumbling along over the river. 'I wanted it to be my idea, my thing. I particularly didn't want to talk to my father about it. The Tinker happened to be here at the time so the obvious thing was to go and talk to them. They were moored up in the river, not so far away, and they were doing some business with us so it was easy to hitch a ride over. You've seen pictures of the Tinker?'

Josh nodded.

'Doesn't prepare you for the real thing. She's massive, one of the biggest ships to ever float. Her deck is so big that you could fly planes off it, but all that space is gone now, buried under factories and workshops. She's hollowed out inside and filled with the same. She's a floating factory the size of a city.'

'Sounds amazing. I thought you'd be trying to put me off,' smiled Josh.

'I will. Don't worry. Anyway, I told them what I had in mind and they sent one of their Foremen with me to take a look at the towers. It soon seemed that the growing mats wouldn't be that hard to do, but he was just as interested in the water system and the interior floors. Looking back, I should have seen something wasn't quite right but… I was young,' and Rodger shrugged.

They could see the pale towers of their Clan House now. 'We're nearly there,' said Josh.

'I know. There's not much more. They started working on the mats and the hoists and the irrigation for them but only Tinker crew were working on it and it felt like they didn't want me around. It didn't feel right and I got more and more worried so eventually I went to my father. I told him what I'd done. You can imagine his reaction.' Josh pulled a face. 'He got some of the clan together and a bunch of farmboys and we went down there. We broke in from the ground floor and climbed an inside stair well. We found out what they were doing. They had put in the growing racks without saying anything. The hydroponics were already installed on more than a dozen floors but that wasn't the worst of it.'

'What? What had they done?'

'Chemz. They were using chemz and fertilizers. It was the old heresy. Growing with science. Some of the chemz got into the irrigation for the mats and that was how we knew. Some of the mat crops had grown huge, but hideous and deformed. It almost kicked off there and then but my father calmed everyone down. At the end of the day, we needed each other.'

'Did they say why they had done it?'

'Because they could. Because the science said that it would work and they had an opportunity to see if they could make it work and, if the Tinker made the tech and it could grow its own food… '

'They would have all the power. They could hold us to ransom and there would be nothing we could do about it.'

'I know. Don't think I haven't thought about that every day since then. But do you know what? Mostly I think they did it just because they could.'

Rodger flew them low over the river, the wing-beat downdraft causing ripples in the mud. With a deft touch he slid the BEE into the main hall and put her down on her pad.

'Think it over. Talk to your Grandpa and get his view. We'll talk some more tomorrow.'

Josh sucked at his teeth. 'Yeah,' he said. 'We will. It's some tale.'

'And slaughter those lambs and get them to the butcher. The farmboys will give you a hand. I'm looking forward to a roast,' and Rodger slid out of his seat and walked off into the depths of the hall.

·

The following morning Rodger came down into the kitchen and found the percolator already on. The room smelt of wood-smoke and coffee. Josh was playing with baby while

Precious put more wood on the fire. They sat together on the warm brick hearth, quiet and companionable.

'Morning, Da,' said Precious.

'Morning, Da,' said Josh.

'Morning, you lot,' said Rodger smiling at the three of them as he walked over to the percolator and poured himself a mug. 'Did you speak to Grandpa?'

'Yeah. Yeah I did,' said Josh.

'And?'

'Well, I think he's mostly forgiven you.'

Rodger laughed quietly.

'Did you two get a chance to talk yesterday?' asked Precious.

'I thought I was supposed to be listening,' replied Rodger. 'But yeah, we did, didn't we?'

'Yeah. We did. And it was good, I think.' Josh bounced the baby on his knee. It giggled and wriggled as he pulled funny faces. 'Don't frighten him,' said Precious and Josh frowned at her. 'I'm not.'

'So are you still running away to sea?' she asked.

Josh sighed. 'It isn't that simple. I've been thinking about it and there could be an adventure right here, if I can persuade him,' said Josh nodding at his father.

'There are lots of adventures I'd like you to stay and help me with, but not with what we saw yesterday. Not that one.'

The new firewood caught and flames blossomed in the hearth like red and yellow flowers. Rodger came and squatted down next to his children. In the background they could hear the small noises of the rest of the household waking up. A dull rumble as pumps started to run water to the washrooms and showers, the clatter of pots in the kitchens, the whole family yawning and stretching and beginning the new day.

'So what do you think?' Rodger asked Josh.

'The thing is, it's what I've dreamed of my whole life, isn't it? Lundun full of people again. Showing the ancients we can do what they did.'

'The ancients won't be here to see and I don't know they'd like it anyway.'

'We'll know how to do it better this time.'

'I guess that's what people always say, just before it all goes wrong again. What did Grandpa say?'

'That you shouldn't have gone behind the fam's back and the Tinker shouldn't have abused your trust, even if you were wrong to give them it in the first place.'

Rodger chewed at his lip. 'Yeah, that's probably about right.'

Precious rocked the swaddled baby on her knee as she listened to the conversation bounce to and fro.

'But there's a bigger question, isn't there?'

'What's that?'

'That growing system could produce more food from one floor than we can get from all our other places put together. We could grow enough food to feed thousands of people. Given time we could grow enough to bring Lundun back to life.'

'What are you talking about?' said Precious. 'What do you call this? This is life. This is our life,' she said with an edge to her voice. She leant over and took the baby out of Josh's hands. She hugged him to her breast.

Josh scowled. 'Lundun used to be home to ten million people.'

'And now it's home to us,' she said, cuddling the baby

protectively. 'Do you think this one wants ten million brothers and sisters or do you think he wants to grow up in the fam surrounded by people he knows and loves?'

'If we turned the hydroponics back on it would still take time. There wouldn't be that many people even in his lifetime, nothing like.'

'How do you think that makes it better? We would have started walking down that road, wouldn't we?' said Rodger and his voice trembled with emotion. 'It would be our legacy. That's not how I want to be remembered.'

'Don't seem you two can agree on anything today,' said Precious.

'Possibly not.'

'You could be right.'

'Well, it sounds to me like you should just do some more listenin' and talkin', but don't forget that you're choosing the future that this one grows up in. Do what's best for him, eh?'

For a moment there was just the crackling of the fire and the slow drip of the percolator. Rodger watched Precious playing with her child. 'What are you trying to do?' he asked. Precious was holding the baby up so that his toes just brushed against the floor. 'I'm trying to get him to stand,' she said.

'He wasn't even very good at sitting yesterday. It's not what he's best at.'

'You're best at being cute, aren't you,' said Precious and tickled the baby under his chin, making him gurgle happily.

'Got a name yet?'

'No. It's so hard to choose. Somethin' that's really him, eh. Captures his spirit. Know what I mean?'

Rodger and Josh nodded. They looked at the swaddled infant, balanced on his nappy-padded butt like a skittle, and they watched as he chuckled and gurgled and slowly, oh so slowly, fell over on to one side.

Josh looked at Rodger and Rodger looked at Josh and they realised that they both had the same thought strike them at the same time.

'He should be called…' and then they both said, 'Topple.'

# AFTERWORD

YOU KNOW that 'tricky' second book; that difficult follow-up to the first one?

This is it.

And it was. Tricky, that is.

I finished writing the last story for this collection in April 2021, two years and two months after Silverback (my first collection of short fiction) was published.

I didn't expect it to take that long.

I didn't expect to squeeze out stories like toothpaste from a tube but I thought, as I had more experience, there was a fighting chance that all would go well.

And up to a point, it did.

I had enjoyed getting *Silverback* finished. There was a sense of achievement and a sense of pride and most importantly, I was hearing that people were enjoying the reading of it.

That was great because I had enjoyed the writing of it.

I like sitting in front of a keyboard or a blank sheet of paper and chronicling what comes into my head. I like the process of choosing the right words to do that with, when to be tricksy and when to be plain. I like going back and reading the rhythm in the words and making it a beat that you can sway along to. I like the craft as much as I enjoy the act of creation.

I was lucky, my father taught me to play with words. To treat them as Lego bricks you could make a world out of or use them to decorate a tune and make a comic song. We used to sit around the dinner table on Sunday and do just that while my mother looked on, perplexed.

So I was looking forward to being at my desk and staring into the imaginarium again, waiting for the first hint of an idea.

Of course, I don't sit there waiting for very long. Not because I am so slick or productive with my inventiveness but that I know that once I've told myself I am in search of an idea, I need to go off and do something else while my subconscious looks for it, or listens for it, or sniffs the breeze.

And usually what happens is that two things hidden away in my memory or sitting in front of me in my day bump together. One of those things might be a chewed old stick but the other is a temple bell and between the pair of them they make an entrancing sound, a note worth following.

So I decide to see where that journey might lead.

Some people say, and I agree with them, that truly original thought is a rare beast and not even one that is always welcome at the feast. Creative thinking and new ideas are more often than not the result of seeing a new connection between things, one that hasn't been seen before, so the more things that interest a person, the more broad a view someone has on the world, the more of these connections they are likely to make and the more original those connections will be. To my mind, people these days specialise too much, they know a great deal about a tightly defined subject. Like a Mastermind contestant on their specialist round they know all there is to know about *England's foreign policy, 1816 to 1820* or *The use of AI in the optimization of offline marketing channels*. I am no big fan of specialisation. I like generalists. Even my short fiction dabbles its toe in the waters of more than one genre.

When I worked in advertising in the eighties, the industry was centred on Soho, an area that was vibrant and culturally diverse. The streets themselves were making connections that were unusual – an ironmonger sat between a strip club and a bakery, an Irish bar was beneath a music company and neighbour to a haberdashery. There was energy, a variety and diversity there and as you walked through Soho it showed you how to be creative, how to mix things up in a way that would surprise and delight.

But 2020 threw a particular spanner into those works for me.

The stories in *Viscera* were written during the time of the pandemic, during a time of lockdown after lockdown.

The pandemic was everywhere.

"Pestilence didn't spread across the world riding a pale horse; rather it travelled by 737 and Airbus. It arrived more quickly that way. Pestilence walked through arrivals with a mild temperature and a duty free bottle of whisky." *The Hedgerows and the Aisles*

It's impossible to think about the writing of the stories that are in this collection without thinking about the pandemic.

I wasn't out and about seeing new things and enjoying new experiences. Like everyone else I was sitting at home in front of my computer trapped in a miasma of memories, fake news and social media trends.

And so that, in part, is what these stories are spun from. We mould the clay that we have to hand but not every pot that's thrown on the wheel…

Well, you get the picture.

I started way more stories than I finished. Some were just a few words but many of them had become thousands of words long before they were spiked; put to one side like a piece of news that isn't going to make the front page.

And I'm not sure why that happened. I found the pandemic stressful and I was certainly more prone to anxiety than I usually am but I'm not sure how that could have resulted in an inability to bring a story to a fitting end.

I suspect it was because ability and expectation are seldom in step. I think the expectations that I had for those stories were higher than my ability to write them. Every journey was going to end up in disappointment, no matter what. But I continued writing. Sometimes the writing was a blessing and sometimes it was a burden, but it was something that I did every day.

And one day that started to pay off.

Having spent months and months learning how not to finish a story in a satisfactory way, one day I typed the very last word and it was done.

And that's another thing about writing into the dark. You are never quite sure what the end is going to be or where it's going to come. Sometimes I get to a moment in the telling of the tale and find that I can't write anymore and only then do I realise that is because the job is done, the story has been told.

And eventually I arrived at the end. Eight tall tales, eight pieces of short imaginative fiction

## THE HEART OF THE SON

I wanted to write a piece of classic sci-fi and this was as close as I got.

Like all good sci-fi, it's very little to do with technology and science and quite a lot to do with characters and relationships.

The title makes me chuckle. It's a riff on the Pink Floyd track, "Set the controls for the heart of the Sun."

And none of the science is made up. The mirror fields, the solar furnace and the molten salt all exist. There are a few such installations around the Med and a couple in the US. Flamers exist too. I wasn't being lazy. It's just that truth is often stranger than fiction and everything seemed to come nicely together and just work so I let it be.

## ROVER

The Mars Perseverance Rover had just been in the news and my original core idea was, 'what if someone sent a vehicle like that to Earth and it was trying to find proof of intelligent life.'

The first test of concept had Rover as an aggressive robot that our hero had to destroy but I had made the conscious decision to make the stories – well, at least some of them – have a slightly more upbeat ending. And the other thing was, as with life, the pandemic insisted on making its presence felt. It became the background to the story and then it became the agency that drove the action.

When I write, I usually write 'into the dark', meaning I don't know how the story is going to end. So it's not unusual for me to find a story changing direction as I'm half way through writing it. That happened to 'Rover'. The idea of the AI being 'dog like' in some way was there from the start but finally getting to 'Fetch' was an evolution of the tale as I sat writing away.

## HARVEST

I live on a farm and each year we make hay. It's something I know about.

When it goes right, it's exciting and when it goes wrong, or is on the cusp of going wrong, when the rain clouds sit on the horizon while the hay bales still sit in the field; that's exciting too.

This particular year things very nearly went wrong. We have never lost a crop of hay since we have lived here but we almost did in 2020 and so I had to write about it.

## LIFECYCLE

Ex-hippies and travellers, people who live on the fringes of society; and it's often quite a tatty and ragged fringe at that. No one seems to write about them and yet for the very reason of their apart-ness they make interesting characters with unusual stories to tell. And I like the idea of the nerd from outer space, the geek from the future.

## THE HEDGEROWS AND THE AISLES

Quite a different piece to the rest, I think.

It captures for me how I felt during that first lockdown. That glorious spring when everyone simply disappeared while the sun shone every day.

It was like entering a dream.

We became untethered from our lives and the world as we had known it and began to float in some strange amniotic fluid made of sunlight and pollen and warm honey and fear. At least, that is how it felt to me.

## LOSING FACE

This is my personal favourite of the three pandemic-influenced tales in the collection.

"I understand your fear of the virus. I myself was infected but not by Covid-19, indeed, not by a respiratory virus at all but by a blood-borne infection and that, a very long time ago." *Losing Face*

The virus and the vampyre; it just seemed such a neat trick and I lived in Seoul for a time and had wanted to write something set in the East and so, once again, the connections all came together rather neatly.

## WISH LIST

Online shopping. I swear at one point there was a delivery guy knocking on my door every single day. We mould the clay that we have to hand.

I am fascinated by the idea of wishes. 'Be careful what you wish for, you just might get it.' 'The Monkey's Paw,' and of course, the genie in the lamp.

For the longest time while I wrote this story it seemed like the Monkey's Paw would be an abiding influence but I eventually decided that I couldn't do anything quite that dark to my characters.

It could still be a cautionary tale without the need for reanimated corpses.

I've always loved the Arthur C. Clarke quote, 'Any sufficiently advanced technology is indistinguishable from magic.' I think that idea is here too, playing its part in the background.

## TOPPLE

Oddly, this began with me wanting to write a story called 'Topple'. Sometimes I just fall in love with a word; the sound of it, the shape of it. Topple is such a word.

And in my mind's eye I saw the baby slowly falling over. And I became a Grandfather this year. And I loved that warm, farmhouse kitchen in the morning vibe the story begins with. But we couldn't have anything as simple as that and I'd been looking at green walls and vertical farming online and so the dots got joined. The connections were made. I could remember reading a Heinlein book called 'Farmer in the Sky' when I was young – like really young – and although I had no recollection of the plot at all the title still had resonance.

I rather like the idea of a future that is post-apocalyptic but not dystopian. What is so wrong with imagining the future as a positive place, where sheep are grazing on the

Hammersmith Flyover and mushrooms growing in the Jubilee Line? Perhaps it's no utopia, but I could happily live there.*

Thank you.

Thank you for reading this and thank you for reading these stories. I hope you were rewarded with a thought, an idea or a feeling that will stay with you for some time. Just because it's short fiction, doesn't mean it shouldn't last.

Love to all xx xx